THE AUTOBIOGRAPHY OF YHOSHUA BAR JOSEF THE ANOINTED

THE AUTOBIOGRAPHY OF YHOSHUA BAR JOSEF THE ANOINTED

A progressive christian's interpretation of the life and teachings of jesus christ

DR. RONALD E. FOORE

© 2016 Dr. Ronald E. Foore
All rights reserved.

ISBN: 1536963380
ISBN 13: 9781536963380
Library of Congress Control Number: 2016913987
CreateSpace Independent Publishing Platform
North Charleston, South Carolina

To Nanette and Marissa
The Muses Who Influence My Journey

INTRODUCTION

This book is an attempt to synthesize faith and reason. Mainstream Christian churches in North America are experiencing monumental drops in membership. Depending on the denomination or religion, in the last quarter century, there have been 25–50 percent drops in church attendance and membership in America. In his landmark 2001 book, *Bowling Alone*, Robert Putnam and those who have followed his thesis explained why Americans mostly do not do things communally anymore, such as join bowling leagues, men's clubs and fraternities, churches, civic clubs, and other community groups. American culture has changed. We have emerged as a nation of hermits. We binge watch dozens of hours of shows alone on Netflix, Hulu, or Amazon Prime; we cocoon in our living rooms, playing games with faceless folks on our smartphones; we spend hours reading posts on Facebook, Twitter, and Instagram; and fewer and fewer of us spend time in libraries, as we instantly download books electronically. Most of us exercise by ourselves in gyms or run alone. Communities are closing their speakers' bureaus, and attendance is even down in many sporting venues because people would rather watch the game or match in the comfort of their own homes.

Reasons for church membership declines in the United States are complex. There are some nondenominational churches that are rapidly growing; people can, almost anonymously, enter a church and go right to a seat to experience a video or upstream of a preacher (who may actually be thousands of miles away) or to experience a live band and singing and then quietly drift away without joining, being baptized, or being held accountable for a tithe. Some mainstream churches have dynamic preachers or community-involved programs that continue to draw the faithful. But for the most part, Americans have become disenchanted with the repetition, the failure to intellectually and spiritually engage, or the irrelevance found in some churches. I think that the reasons for mainstream church decline are twofold.

One has to do with the fact that Americans are just smarter about religion and history than they were in the twentieth century. People watch the History Channels (there is more than one now) as well as countless other stations on cable or satellite streaming. They present pretty interesting information about world religions with recent popular shows such as *Beliefs*, by Oprah, and other shows on God or religion narrated by well-known celebrities and movies about the Holocaust (such as *Schindler's List*) where Christians kill Jews in genocides as well as documentaries on the Crusades, the Dead Sea Scrolls, newly uncovered Gospels (such as the Gospel of Judas, for example), and other topics dealing with religious history, which have fanned religious interest. Why go to church to learn about religion, ethics, morality, and interpretations of Jesus's life when there are countless preachers, scholars, theologians, and even seminary professors at the touch of your finger on your remote? Some of the best theological minds are now available on DVD (for example, through *Great Courses*) or lectures can be streamed (sometimes live) from TED Talks.

Another reason is that Americans have become more sophisticated. I don't mean to imply that most Americans have grown up and out of churches, leaving their pews in the dust. It is just that a new paradigm is emerging. As Jesus was fond of pointing out to His disciples, why don't you get it? It takes a lot of thinking to interpret allegories, metaphors, and stories for the betterment of one's life. Not just the overt plot of a narrative (the story of the prodigal son, for example) is important; it is what it can teach us about how we live our lives. I think that compared to a few decades ago, more Americans have experienced college courses or even high school courses that have exposed them to world religions, church history, or world history. Millions of students have successfully taken advanced-placement courses sponsored by the College Board and have had the opportunity to intellectualize areas of philosophy, psychology, and sociology—courses that eluded earlier generations.

I have been a Methodist for sixty-five years, had many years of perfect attendance in Sunday school, regularly attended Methodist Youth Fellowship on Sunday evenings, went to Wednesday-night services, and received years of instruction from the official programs of the church. In my later years, I have acquired a perspective on the development of mainstream Christianity in America. I have taught world religion, history, psychology, sociology, and political-science classes at the college and high school levels. I have attended countless lectures on religion and theology and talked to people from many different beliefs, places, and cultures. I find it difficult to peg my belief, however.

I feel that I want to be and am part of a rebirth being experienced by many faithful Christians. Some of the words used to describe us are *postpartisan, transformational Christians, postmodern, postliberal, progressive, emerging, nontraditional, new paradigm,* or *twenty-first-century Christians.* However, I am labeling myself as a *journey Christian.* I am on a journey of faith. I am not at a destination. I don't have all the answers; in fact, I have more questions than I have answers. I want to cling to my belief because I truly think that there is in all humans the need to experience a metaphysical encounter with the life force or energy we call God. We ask ourselves these questions: From where have we come? Where are we going? How do we get there? We know from psychology that one of the basic needs we express is a sense of belonging. We know that to become self-actualized we must experience a degree of altruism, wonder, and service to others as well as what can only be described as metaphysical wisdom. And I firmly believe that love is the central core of human beings. For me, the core teaching can be found in the way of Jesus.

The Way, the core teaching of Jesus, was summed up in the introductory words of the *Didache,* written only one generation following the crucifixion of Jesus and preceding the widespread dissemination of the Gospels and the epistles of Paul, in the first century CE. "There are two ways, one of life and one of death, but a great difference between the two ways. The way of life, then, is this: First, you shall love God who made you; second, love your neighbor as yourself, and do not do to another what you would not want done to you." The other way, the way of death, is a dark journey filled with hate, jealousy, envy, and guilt. The way of life, then, is love. Over a period of two millennia, over thirty-three thousand different Christian denominations, churches, sects, cults, and religions have been instituted, which have mostly altered, changed, and morphed this simple teaching into sometimes complex, convoluted, and even contradictory beliefs. Love God and love humans. That is the foundation of Jesus's teaching.

Most scholars believe that Jesus historically existed. I am starting with this premise for this book. Obviously, no historical document we are aware of is in the form of His autobiography. At the core of this book is an attempt to present the life and teachings of Jesus, stripped from stories and narratives added over the millennia. I have attempted to present scenes that fall into a plausible picture of Jesus's life, which have been corroborated by nonbiblical sources, such as historical accounts and manuscripts currently available to scholars. This is an attempt to strengthen Christian faith and belief in light of contemporary research and reasonable thought. C.S. Lewis and other apologists have searched their hearts to find an intellectual synergy with Jesus' teachings, free from magic, the supernatural, and the thaumaturgic. This story posits that Jesus lived, he taught, and his teachings can transform the world.

THE AUTOBIOGRAPHY OF YHOSHUA BAR JOSEF THE ANOINTED

A person's life can be a paradox. I set my hand to writing about my life to shed light on the events of my experiences as best as I can. People tell tales and stories about me that are fantastic in scope, glorious in ideas, and mysterious in thoughts. The truth of my life, as I remember it, however, is far more interesting and powerful. In my experience, some people emerge as heroes while others are forgotten in the mists of time. Eyewitness accounts are embellished or elaborated over time, and what really took place becomes obscured. If five, ten, or fifteen people see exactly the same event at the same time and place, they will each have different perspectives on what transpired. People attempt to fill in their gaps in memory with events or spoken words, or they even recreate what people looked like or were wearing. As stories are passed from person to person or among several groups, the accounts of the past become blurred, and they evolve as mere shadows of the original reality. I lived among mostly nomadic, illiterate, and simple people who were dealing with a new paradigm in processing my teaching, and as happens to all figures of history, some things devolved into myth (not intentionally, but that is how the human mind works). It seems as though this has held true for me. People tend to retain the gist of what happened, but getting the details correct is something else. My fervent hope in contemplating my story is that you, the reader, will find enlightenment and faith. But that is up to you to decide.

MY EARLY YEARS

I was born in the time of late summer[7] to loving parents. I have been told and I have heard many stories surrounding the events of my birth, but of course, I have no memories of the earliest times of my life. My father, Josef, was, according to our family's traditions, a descendent of the fabled Hebrew king David's line of the family of Judah. Josef was much older than my mother was and was well respected in our community. By the time of my birth, there were hundreds if not thousands of men and women who could claim David as their ancestor, but knowing my lineage made me feel a special kinship with my Jewish heritage. I grew up thinking that royal blood from the tribe of Judah flowed through my veins, and this bolstered my confidence as I faced the routine hurdles of childhood. In my later years of life, all the families (I knew of at least six of these families, but there were many more) associated with King David were held suspect by Roman rulers, and because of the Messianic stories that circulated about me and others, many of my extended family and relatives were watched closely by authorities or persecuted. My mother, Miriam, once told me that she too was descended from royalty. She was from the tribe of Levi, and she had been told that one of her ancestors was the great leader Aaron. I never knew my maternal grandparents, Joachim and Anna, as they were very old when my mother was born and died soon after my birth. This ancestry doubled my royal heritage and gave me great satisfaction. But this inner satisfaction carried with it a strong responsibility as well, as we shall later see.

My parents were not poor but self-sufficient. We lived in a small, unimportant nomadic settlement called En-nazira,[12] which was one of some very small Galilean villages clustered together. En-nazira was a barren, rocky, dry, and desolate place in what was then called northern Judea. There were few shrubs and no trees, and to make water wells and cisterns, the people had to dig through solid rock to quite great depths. Our settlement consisted of a few dozen families who attempted to live their simple lives as herders of goats or craftsmen. There were two larger towns within walking distance from my village, and many of the men of En-nazira worked as day laborers from sunrise to sundown, toiling through hot and dusty days. My father was a master stonemason.[1] Some might call him a builder or a kind of architect. He enjoyed a good reputation as a hard worker and skilled craftsman.

My earliest memories start, as most people's do, when I was about four years old. My first recollections are playing in the hot dirt during the day with simple toys and playthings and trying to stay warm inside during the cold nights. Our dwelling was only one room that was surrounded by crudely cut rocks, which had been carefully pieced together to form walls. Our house had one door, which was covered at night and in the winter months with a large blanket. We had no windows. Our floor was simply the dirt we had packed down on occasion by stomping our feet in the entryway, and in the rear of our house was a raised stone platform where we slept and ate. Our roof was constructed from some thin, woody sycamore crossbeams, covered with brushwood, thatched, and then covered with mud. Our roof was always a green color because of the sprouting seeds in the mud. We were constantly repairing the roof, and during seasonable months, we sometimes slept atop it under the stars. The only other hole in our walls was situated by our indoor oven, which allowed for the escape of smoke. We burned charcoal, dried animal manure, and grass as well as whatever brush we could buy or pick up for our cooking and heat, and the inside of our house most times smelled of burning ash, charcoal, and cinders. Our interior was lit with an olive-oil lamp with a flaxen wick. We always had salted fish, fruits, bread, and vegetables from our small garden; chickens that provided us with eggs; and goats too. As many people did, we had constructed some underground chambers for our house where we stored items, but we had few decorative things, as virtually all the items found in our home were useful in our day-to-day living. My mother was always happy, singing and telling me stories, and she taught me, over the years, to enjoy life.

MY CHILDHOOD

My early childhood was one of loving kinship with my parents and brothers and sisters. My brothers were James, Justus (sometimes called Joseph, James the Younger, or Joses), Jude (sometimes called Trionus, Lebbaeus, Thaddaeus, or Judas), and Simon (sometimes called Simeon), and my sisters were named Miriam (sometimes called Mary) and Sophia (sometimes called Salome).[2] Our family was devout and happy, and I have fond memories of play and enjoyment with my siblings. One of the most steadfast family members throughout my entire life and my best childhood friend was a great-uncle by marriage, named Joseph, who lived in a neighboring town in Judea called Ha-Ramathaim or Ramathaim-Zophim by the Judeans of the day but which is called Arimathea by others. Joseph was two years older than I was, which others laughed about because he was a brother of my great-aunts Bianca and Ann (my mother's mother). His elderly father was a prosperous trading merchant who owned several sea-going ships and who traded with farmers, traders, and tin miners in faraway places. Joseph's mother had been quite a bit younger than his father was and had died during childbirth. This family also owned or sponsored many shops in several towns as well as in the bazaar in Jerusalem, which allowed for the sale of trade goods. Joseph would relate many of the tales and stories told to him by his father about his journeys, and we often incorporated these narratives into our play as we sought hidden treasure in mysterious places, fought sea pirates and robbers, and were eager to learn more about the world beyond life as we knew it.

    I learned when I became older that my father was considered a masterful stonemason and craftsman. He had spent his youth apprenticed to a member of one of the guilds from a nearby village, and he was taught to read and the necessary computation skills important to masonry and to building. He did much of his work in a larger town nearby, called Sepphoris, where he assisted in the building of a temple and houses. He would return at night from his labors, usually quite exhausted and worn out from his day's toils. Because of the wages resulting from his skills, we were always able to have enough to eat, and our house was one of the best constructed in our little settlement. My father's friends and family members would drop in on a regular basis, and I enjoyed listening to their conversations as the fire crackled on cool evenings. The quiet calmness of my father's voice seemed to reassure me.

In time, my father began to teach me to read. He brought home some simple scrolls he acquired from friends, and we worked together for hours, learning the words and phrases and how they represented ideas. Using the level, ruler, and other tools as metaphors for the tools needed to create a wise and happy life, he taught me important lessons. In some ways, this was the best part of my youth—sitting next to my father and learning, asking questions, and thinking, which became almost an obsession for me. When my learning outpaced the knowledge of my father, he sent me for tutoring to a schoolmaster named Zaccheus in a nearby village. After spending time with me and initially teaching me about reading and writing, he realized that I had already been provided with more than a basic education, so he proceeded to add new subjects to my studies, including astronomy, rhetoric, and mathematics.

I relished the times my family and friends would travel to the temple in Jerusalem. When I visited Jerusalem, I marveled at the Herodian walls, Herod's temple and palace, and the Antonia Fortress. Obedient Jews would go to temple celebrations three times each year: at the time of Passover, which tied to the Feast of the Unleavened Bread immediately following, Pentecost, and the Feast of the Tabernacles. These were wonderful opportunities for me to experience the life of a city, converse with rabbis, and listen to the stories of other visitors.

As time passed, my father and I realized that I seemed to have a knack for reading and ciphering. I had no interest in pursuing stonework as my vocation, and my family realized that I yearned for a more scholarly and spiritual life. I enjoyed talking to and listening to adults discussing matters of religion, the law, the history of our people, and village gossip. I studied with many groups of teachers in nearby villages and towns, including the Pharisees and Sadducees. As a child, I grew quite confident and yearned for more knowledge. By the time I was eight years old, my father had made arrangements with a nearby group of scholars and holy men who were called by others Essenes. Their encampment was several miles away from En-nazira, toward the north of the Dead Sea. When my cousin John became an orphan at the death of his elderly parents, Elizabeth and Zechariah, he had been taken in by these Essenes, and he was thriving. So, reluctantly, my parents allowed me to live with this group also. In exchange, I did menial jobs and helped repair dwellings, and by the time I was eleven, I was teaching younger children. Life in the Essene encampment was very harsh compared to my life back at home, but I flourished within the learning environment.

MY ESSENE INFLUENCE

Our little community had many visitors who came to stay with us from time to time. We gave them food and shelter. I learned that charity to all who ask is one of the more important practices in life. I learned that property and material goods were best thought of as belonging to all people. I was taught the importance of purity and that living a simple monastic life separate from the mundane routines of regular life can help sharpen skills related to the mind. The rabbis in my Essene village provided me the opportunity to read sacred texts and ask questions. I basked in the knowledge and wisdom afforded to me and learned much. My Essene teachers placed great importance on me being a descendent of King David, and my cousin John and I quickly formed a nucleus of students who bonded through searching for light. We were counseled by our elders that because of whom we were great things would be expected from us.

Some of the teachers began to speculate that my cousin John could become a prophet, as was written about in the book of Malachi. This prophet would pave the way for a major rabbi.[3] My teachers in my Essene village talked about a messiah for our people—a man who would lead us to overcome the plight of Roman rule over our land so we might become the masters of our own destinies. As I grew older, many of my rabbis began to refer to me as the new teacher of righteousness. This title bewildered me, but in my later years, I contemplated its meaning a lot. We were taught the skills of interpretation, analysis, ciphering, and oratory as well as history, and a great deal of our time was spent praying, reading, and conversing with our teachers. John, my cousin, adopted the ways of the Essenes, becoming a teacher in his own right and incorporating their ideas of baptism, dress, and chastity, but to him, the teachings of the Essenes did not go far enough. He later broke away from them and set out on his own, as did I.

A VISIT TO THE TEMPLE

When I was twelve, my parents took me to the city called Jerusalem to observe the splendid rites of Passover as they did every year. My father had spent some time in Jerusalem as a master craftsman and consulted with fellow guild members who were working on the great temple. This particular instance stands out in my mind, though. As was my custom and because of my reputation as an avid student with the Essenes, I spent a lot of time on these visits sitting close to the rabbis, priests, and their students. I enjoyed listening to the discussions relating to the history of our people and interpreting scriptures, and I often engaged in discussions and debates with others.

On this particular occasion, a very old woman, some called her a prophetess, named Anna approached me and called me aside. She told me that several years earlier, as a young girl, she had visited with my parents on one of their pilgrimages to Jerusalem, and she had held me as a baby and had visited with me later when I was a young boy. She told me that day that she saw a sense of knowing in my eyes and felt a sense of serenity as she looked down on me. She told me that she had conferred with a friend of hers, a man named Simeon, who was also a holy man, and they marveled at how I seemed to be so wise at such a young age. The teachers at the temple heard her comments, and many took an interest in me as they contemplated what this woman had said. We sat for hours talking, and the teachers' glances among themselves swelled me with great pride as we carried on lengthy discourses. I had learned much from my Essene tutors, and the teachers gathered at the temple were greatly enjoying our talks. I told the rabbis all about my early ideas about the law, precepts, and statutes and the mysteries that seemed to be contained in the books of the prophets. I discussed with them how a writer could relate a simple story but that story might be analyzed on more than one deeper level to reveal truths beyond the surface. As we conversed, sometimes rabbis and students would break away from our discourse and begin their own discussions and debates about scriptures and interpretations, building on our conversations.

I remember, though, how time got away from us and how my parents showed up following what, unknown to me, had been a frantic search for me. They were appreciative of the teachers for watching over me, but as we left, I remember how these teachers thanked me, telling me how they welcomed my insights. One even referred to me as "rabbi." It was an exhilarating experience. It was at this time that a seed seemed to have been planted in my mind. I enjoyed teaching. I enjoyed offering my insights and ideas, and I relished the conversations I had. There seemed to be no more important role for me than to become a teacher, and this marked one of the most important events of my life.

A MOVE TO EGYPT

After our return to Galilee, my father realized that there was little work to be had in that area. Construction work was very hard to come by, as there was a very bad drought all over our land. Our small settlement of Ennazira was falling away since jobs became scarce, and my family was faced with a decision about where to go. Many of our neighbors were packing for moves elsewhere, and there was little to keep us there. My mother had relatives who lived far away in Egypt, and so we, as a family, elected to pick up and travel far to the southwest, seeking work and a new life. Our trek southward took us to a port city where my father paid for our passage to Egypt. We traveled across water (it was the first time I had experienced life on a ship) and walked a long distance across land to the city of Osyrhynchus, where my father and mother were welcomed by relatives. We lived in Egypt for the next ten years. I cannot begin to tell about the experiences I had growing up to manhood in this wonderful area. While we were surrounded by people of Hebrew culture all the while, observing strict Jewish religious rites, I was able to walk the city streets, talking to people from many different beliefs, backgrounds, and origins. I met people from seemingly all over the world.

As I grew into manhood, I became friends with folks from lands I had previously never heard of, such as India, Britannia, Hispania, Axum, Germania, Cyrenaica, and Greece. I learned much from listening and observing the ways of speaking and socializing, and I studied how other cultures worshipped and thought about God. Some people believed that there were many gods, each of whom had specific and particular powers, influences, and responsibilities. I became fascinated with how individual cities and tribes worshipped their own gods and goddesses, erected statues and likenesses of these deities, and even carried figurines and iconic doll-like amulets made from wood, ivory, or rock in the folds of their clothes. My uncle and best friend, Joseph, visited about once every fourteen or sixteen months as he accompanied his father on business to Osyrhynchus, as he too had relatives who lived there. We bolstered our friendship by continuing to talk about our teenage experiences, and I enjoyed learning that he had married and was set to inherit his father's business.

While in Osyrhynchus, I earned small sums of money working as an apprentice stonemason and carpenter, sometimes alongside my father, doing small jobs in the many holy temples and shrines that were located in this city. I was extremely interested in the subject of religion, and while working on these small jobs, I was afforded the opportunity to talk to other workers, temple laborers, and assistants to the priests. There were many temples to Egyptian deities, such as Osiris, Serapis, Atargatis-Bethnnis, and Hera-Isis. There were Greek temples devoted to Dionysus, Apollo, Demeter, and Hermes, as well as Roman temples and shrines for Jupiter Capitolinus and Mars. I developed a strong sense of the need among people to turn over their troubles and afflictions to a higher power and trust in the wisdom that there are forces of nature as well as metaphysical ideals that govern a higher scheme of life beyond what humans can understand. I honed my relationship with my heavenly Father and prayed for hours at a time.

I learned that there were good and honest people who had grown up with different interpretations of religion. People seemed to have a universal need to make sense out of life. Why are we here? Where do we go when we die? What is the purpose of human life? Why do bad and terrible things happen to good and godly people? Why sometimes do dishonest and bad people become successful and even rise to positions of power? Who or what is God? What are the limits placed upon us as we live close to others? Is it always a sin to tell a lie? Is it always wrong to steal, even if done to provide food for people who are starving? Why is there illness?

THE AUTOBIOGRAPHY OF YHOSHUA BAR JOSEF THE ANOINTED

Is God in heaven really still punishing humans for the sins of Adam and Eve, who lived so very long ago? Why should innocent people who have done no wrong be punished for something that they did not do? What do other people think about the stories I have been taught? Were the events that existed in the Hebrew scriptures real-life happenings, or were they more like stories with multilayered meanings? Could I learn anything from their stories? I became like a sponge, absorbing all this information while praying for answers. I learned to speak in several different languages other than my native Aramaic and could read and write in Greek as well as in other tongues.

While in this Egyptian city, I first became acquainted with papyrus and discovered many writings. I spent some time talking to scribes who allowed me to read poems, government papers, and business forms, such as receipts and tax records. Since my father had earned his credentials as a master craftsman, he easily was invited to become a member of the local builders' guild, and I accompanied him to several locations as he completed his work. Some of the small jobs I performed around the city included working for small-business men.

DEVELOPMENT INTO MANHOOD

When I was twenty-two years old, another chapter in my life closed and a new one began. My father was killed suddenly in an accident related to his work. One of the saddest days of my life was when my family buried this wonderfully gifted man who had taught me much about being strong, working diligently, and loving family. My mother, now faced with life without an income and with seven children, decided to move back to a new home in Judea. We moved in with family members in the area of Galilee, relatives by marriage to my uncle Joseph. Galilee in northern Judea was one of the most beautiful areas of the world I ever saw. Some of Galilee was mountainous, and some of the land was situated by great and wonderful lakes. Because of the abundant rains and fertile lands, this was a haven for many families. The economy was abundant, and our family settled in with great hope for our future. As time passed, my brothers were apprenticed into trades such as carpentry, stonemasonry, and weaving. My sisters, when they came of age, married into caring families. My path took a different direction.

WORLD TRAVELS

My uncle Joseph asked me if I wanted to travel with him and his aging father as they went on some trade missions. I eagerly accepted, and for the next eight years of my life, I sailed to some of the most fascinating places in the world. We would take goods produced in the region of Galilee, such as various trade goods, spices, ointments such as nard, jewelry, olive oil, wheat, pulses, wines, wood products, pottery, and dyes, and transport these items to other lands where we traded for goods to bring back. Joseph and his family would trade anything worthwhile, but we never involved ourselves in the trade of slaves. We would sail to Greece where we traded for such items as Corinthian bronze (which I am proud to say was used to help form the temple gates in Jerusalem). From Lebanon, we brought back wood timbers made from cedar; from the areas around Sidon and Tyre, we purchased glassware and purple dye; from Cypress, we returned with figs; and from Babylonia, we brought woven textiles and finely constructed white linen called byssus.

We traveled frequently to Mesopotamia for pepper and other spices; to Persia for beautiful vases and rugs; to India for linen; and to Arabia for frankincense, cinnamon, and cassia. We traveled south to Axum, which was a kind of crossroad for caravans from lands far to the east, from all parts of Africa, and from many other faraway places. From Britannia, we traded for tin from mines near the Brue River. We continued to trade with our Egyptian friends and family contacts from whom we purchased corn. Traders would come to Galilee from Medes, Phrygia, Cos, Galatia, Pisidia, Cilicia, Cappadocia, Syria, Axum, Asia, Pamphylia, Rome, Gaul, and Libya to barter for goods with our family.

When we arrived in ports, after I assisted Joseph and other workers in unloading goods from our ships, I spent time talking to local holy men, priests, and scholars about their gods, rituals, ceremonies, beliefs, and ideas. I learned about navigation and learned how to read charts. I learned new languages and quickly became a kind of translator between the people with whom we were trading, mostly using Greek or Arabic, and us as tools for communication. By my time, Hebrew was already a dead language, only spoken in the temple or in religious ceremonies, so it and my native Aramaic were of little use in talking to people of other places.

I spent time watching and learning from shamans, healers, and men well versed in the use of medicines, herbs, and ointments in helping cure the sick. I learned about the necessity of the patient wanting to be healed, having a positive attitude, and having faith in the healer, especially in instances when mental fatigue, anxiety, fear, and guilt existed in the person's mind. I learned that many afflictions of the body—such as seizures, mental illness, rashes, and diseases of the bowel and heart—could be caused by worry and stress. I was taught how to measure a pulse and to count breaths and how the eyes, nails, and tongue can help diagnose illnesses. I discovered how certain tree barks, berries, teas, soups, insects, and plants could help heal the sick. I witnessed seemingly miraculous cures of patients in many places through using serenity, prayer, calmness, and tranquility. I learned much about how a person's relationship with his or her god, family, and him- or herself decided that person's own physical as well as spiritual well-being. I learned about and taught others about the healing power of prayers. I became aware that at least one-third of all illnesses are really diseases of the soul or of a troubled mind, and if people truly believed that they could be healed, then a large percentage of those afflicted with illness, what some people called demons, could be cured. I became a healer in my own right, putting into practice the lessons I learned from my many teachers and my God-given ability to make practical use of the ideas to which I had been exposed.

I was able to formulate a plan for my life, which included preaching the truths as I knew them to be, using the knowledge and wisdom gained from study, listening, analyzing, and praying to my Father in heaven. We are surrounded by miracles every day of our lives if we only take the time to watch and listen. Too often, we are in too much of a hurry to stop and experience the essence of the life of which we are all part. The life force in all plants, animals, insects, and even inanimate substances, such as rocks, sand, and the air we breathe, all have profound effects on us as we live out our lives. For every good thing that we do, think, say, or create, an ongoing wave of purity and goodness is created that stems from our actions. These have ripple effects in space and time. Likewise, each of our bad or evil thoughts and actions can have rippling consequences that affect other people and the world around us. Through untold hours on the decks of our ships, sailing from place to place, or on camels, walking long distances on land, I spent hundreds of hours praying, formulating my thoughts, and thinking about how best I could use my life for the glory of my Father God and for the benefit of my fellow men and women.

God and prophets came to me in my dreams where I envisioned how my life pathways might turn. I could take an easy route and remain with my uncle Joseph as he grew into a successful merchant. I could return to Galilee and take up my late father's stone-craftsman labors, or I could follow the path that grew clearer and clearer to me as time passed—to do my Father's work as a child of God, to teach, to heal, and to urge people to become better. I had found many temptations as I ventured with my uncle Joseph to bedazzling parts of the world. I encountered temptations of the flesh, temptations of the heart, and temptations of the mind. I observed my fellows when they became embroiled in debauchery and scandal, and I observed how men would mislead and lie to each other and steal and rob for their own personal gain. More than once, our ships or caravans were set upon by thieves, and we had to defend our persons and our merchandise from these evildoers. Eventually, I emerged out of the hellish world in which I sometimes found myself, and I sought an inner peace through communion with my God and vowed to attempt to live the most pious life I could while helping others.

PREPARATION FOR PREACHING

In the thirtieth year of my life, I bid farewell to my uncle Joseph and our adventures, and I returned to Galilee to visit our family and friends. Joseph's father had passed away, and with the inheritance of his father's many business and trading ventures, my uncle continued to greatly prosper; he eventually became a man of great wealth and social prestige as well as high standing within the political and religious communities as a member of the prestigious Sanhedrin, the governing body of priests for my people. As time passed, my uncle Joseph was designated an assistant to the Roman decurion and eventually was elevated to the position of decurion himself, which was a great position likened to a minister of mines, since he was instrumental in the procurement of vast amounts of tin from his contacts in Glastonbury Isle in the south of Britannia.

My mother and brothers observed my deep introspections and urged me to travel to visit my cousin John's encampment in an effort to calm my soul. John had left the Essene village we had both inhabited as youths, and he had proceeded to lead an ascetic life in the desert. He had slowly earned a reputation as a holy man, and several people lived closely with him wherever he went. I visited friends and relatives in the areas in which I had spent my childhood, went to our synagogue and read aloud from the scroll of Isaiah, and sat with those present. I tendered my interpretations of what I had read to them, and they seemed to marvel at my ideas. Reading our Isaiah scroll was not an easy task, for it was very long with over fifteen panels of goatskin, which were sewn together. The scroll was always rolled from the right to the left, and it was always placed upon a table while unrolling and reading. Our religion was fairly simple and could be summed up with four ideas: God, our land, the Torah, and our people. Throughout my adult life, I always wore a tzitzit, which was a fringed tassel on the outside of whatever garment I was wearing. It served to show others my observance of the commandments of the Torah, called by us the *mitzvoth*. I would always appreciate the respect afforded to me in the area of my hometown, and I often told my followers that prophets are sometimes not without honor except in their home village among their relatives and in their own houses.

JOHN THE BAPTIZER

Following great prayer, I followed my heart and sought out John, who was now referred to as "the Baptizer." John was roaming the countryside with a band of followers, teaching about a coming Messiah who would prepare the way for an apocalyptic judgment. John was baptizing a growing number of followers, which was emerging as a rite of the forgiveness of sin in preparation for future events. His followers were calling themselves the people of "the Way," and John was beginning to see his role as just like the old prophet Elijah's was.

    I went to visit with John when he was near Bethany in Perea, along the Jordan River, in the forty-sixth year of the construction of the temple in Jerusalem and, with his followers, listened to him preach. John was what used to be called a "Nazirite," or a person who had chosen to live a separate life. He had let his hair and beard grow long and unkempt, and he wore a cloak made of the skin of a camel. He ate only what the desert provided and a kind of cake made from stray plants with wild honey. John, who was only separated from me in birth by six months, was a great preacher who had a motivating way with his words, elegantly and eloquently instilling a kind of revolutionary zeal into the minds and hearts of all who heard him. John preached and ministered to his followers and often stated that if a person had two coats, let him share with him who had none, and he who had food let him do likewise. In my heart, I felt a readiness for change with what John had been preaching and realized that this radical fire was also in me—a kind of need to fill a void in my soul.

    I wanted to make a public demonstration of my willingness to be born anew in the spirit of God, to bring about a change and direction in my life.

THE AUTOBIOGRAPHY OF YHOSHUA BAR JOSEF THE ANOINTED

I approached John and asked if he might baptize me. I remember a faraway look crossing his face. He replied so that others could hear that maybe I should baptize him. I replied in a loud voice that among those born of women, none was greater than John was. We laughed, and then we looked into each other's eyes and became very serious. He counseled me that with my baptism, I would become a new person. My life would be changed; my old life would end in a way because my soul would now belong to God, and I would become filled with a holy and sacrosanct spirit. With this change would come responsibilities and a new direction for my life. We prayed together, as we had done many times before during our childhood, growing up in the Essene village surrounded by our elders and fellow students. We were both men of destiny, however, and this moment seemed like none other I had ever experienced. We walked out into the water, and he submerged my whole body, praising God and praying that the spirit of the Lord would enter my soul, my mind, and my body. I held my breath, closed my eyes, and let the cool splashing of the water engulf me. In a way, I felt the sins of my life pass from me.

In my mind and in my heart, I felt cleansed of my transgressions and my sloppy and humble attempts to live my life alone. Others and I perceived the act of baptism as a kind of purification. As I was raised up, it was as if I were a new man. Upon rising from the water, I heard a voice, and to this day, I do not know who it was, whether it was John or somebody else, say, "This is my beloved son with whom I am well pleased." My ears were still full of water, and my eyes were bleary, but my heart fluttered like the wings of a dove with excitement. As I emerged from the water, the first thing I saw was that John's eyes were full of tears, and there was a smile on his lips. It was quite a sight to see John, as he wore the clothes of a pauper and his hair was long and dirty. He was not known for his humor or laughter, and to see him smiling was a new experience. Many of John's followers witnessed my baptism as well as a large group of onlookers who happened to be present at the river that day.

John announced to the crowd that had assembled around us that I was the "lamb of God," and this had a profound effect on me. I had been prepared for a new direction for my life, but I needed some time to reflect on a plan on how to carry it out. Two young men who would become two of my most loving and devoted followers were also present that day at my baptism; Andrew, son of Jonas, was a fisherman by trade and a disciple of my cousin, the baptizer, and John bar Zebedee was also a fisherman and a disciple of my cousin John's. The new friend, whose name, again, was John, was actually our cousin too, since he was one of the sons of Zebedee, a fisherman of Galilee, and his mother, Salome, was sister to my mother (and thus my aunt). These two men approached me and told me that their hearts were filled with allegiance and fealty toward me when they witnessed my baptism, and they wished to now follow me in my new path. We talked all night long, and along with John (the Baptizer), we decided that it would be best if I took some time to work things out in my mind. After prayer and further discussion, I decided to go by myself, alone, to the desert to sort things out.

ALONE IN THE DESERT

I went out alone into the desert and wandered around for a month and ten days. It was hot and dry, and I became thirsty and hungry. I had taken nothing with me for provisions or water, wanting to clear my mind and spirit for what was to come, similar to the example set by my cousin John. God provided for me as I walked, sat, made my primitive camps, and reflected. I found water in the form of dew on the leaves of plants in the early morning hours or in small puddles made by digging into the earth near where plants were growing. I hardly ate anything and lost a lot of weight. At times, I saw visions and heard voices. I dreamed that an evil demon was talking to me. In one dream, this evil tempted me to break my fast and eat. I responded to the evildoer that as my people fasted in the desert in the time of Moses, I too would observe their suffering and not eat. In another dream, I was tempted to become the warlike Messiah for whom the people of Israel were searching, to lead them out of the bondage of the rule by the Romans. Might the purpose of my life be to organize a revolt, to establish a new kingdom, and to become a rich and powerful king? I rebuked this notion by citing my will to live a humble life and to help others. In a third dream, the Evil One came to me and asked me to put my Father God to a test, but I remembered the story of how Moses rebuked the Israelites for testing God, and I challenged this reasoning.

    I came out of this time in the desert with renewal and a plan. These visions and others that would occur could serve my purposes by helping me relate stories as parables. For example, when I told of my visions of evil, the temptations might be viewed as warnings not to be nervous about worldly needs, not to fret over death, and not to aspire for total political power or revolt. I realized that people need, first and foremost, a sense of community and belonging. My whole life had been devoted, up to this point, to learning and wisdom, but I was now going to dedicate myself to teaching, healing, and preaching the truths about life as I understood them to be through the directions of my Father God in heaven.

In this time, there were dozens of holy men, rabbis, preachers, and prophets who were wandering the hills and valleys of Judea. One of these men, named Carabbas, had acquired a large following as he walked from one village to another. Some professed to be the Jewish Messiah, some believed themselves to be a new prophet, and some thought that they were the saviors of Israel. I was well aware of these traveling preachers and had heard many of them speak. I had no desire to compete with these other men or to create a groundswell of change within my faith. I felt that I had a different new message to share—one of love, compassion, and forgiveness, so I set about creating the means to do just that.

THE START OF MY QUEST

When I returned to Bethany, I sought out Andrew and John bar Zebedee, and we discussed how I would begin my preaching journey. Andrew, a native of Galilee, born in Bethsaida (his mother was named Joanna, and his father was a fisherman named Jonah or John), had many contacts throughout the region and became one of the most important recruiters to my ministry, even introducing me to his brother, Simon (Peter). Their father, Jonah, was a well-known rabbi and prophet who had lived very near where I grew up in a small settlement called Gath-Hepher. Peter too was a fisherman and lived in Bethsaida and Capernaum. The four of us, my cousin John bar Zebedee, Andrew, his brother Simon Peter, and I, conversed for several days about our plan. My three new friends asked me many questions about my beliefs and ideas and about my life. As the days passed, we walked around Galilee, stirring up much inquiry and excitement as we talked to other people. Soon, others began to join our little group—James (the Elder), the brother of my follower John, who joined our group as we visited him along the Sea of Galilee; Jude (or Thaddeus, sometimes also called Trionius or Lebbaeus, a brother of James the Younger and mine); James (the Younger as he was referred to); Judas (the son of Simon Iscariot, who was the only man in my inner circle of followers who was from Galilee but was from the area of Kerioth in southern Judea); Matthew (sometimes called Levi), son of Alphaeus, who was a tax collector working near Capernaum, a small fishing village on the Sea of Galilee's north shore; Philip (of the tribe of Zebulon); and Bartholomew (sometimes called Nathanael), who was of the royal blood of the king of

Geshur and of the House of Naphtali and the son of Tolmai, introduced to me by Philip. Bartholomew would tell people we would meet along our travels that I was the "Son of God" and the "king of Israel," which made many Jewish leaders anxious. Simon (my brother) was the one whom we called "the Zealot" or "the Canaanite" because he was the only member of our group who had followed the Zealot movement, which had wanted to create a violent overthrow of the Roman rule in our land. Finally, there was Thomas (sometimes known as Didymas, which means twin).

My mother and sisters also accompanied our little band, along with some of the wives, sisters, and daughters of my followers. Our daily needs pertaining to cooking, sewing, and care were always provided. Adding to our little group was another disciple named Mary Madeleine from the fishing village of Magdala and her sister Martha as well as their brother Lazarus and several others. Mary's family was very wealthy, and she and her family gave generously to our group, allowing us to purchase food and lodgings during our travels for the next three years, even allowing us to stay in their houses in Bethany and Magdala when our journey took us near their homes.

A WEDDING AND THE GENESIS OF MY PREACHING

For the next year, John continued to preach in the northern areas of Galilee, the Decapolis, Aenon near Salim, and Perea, while I began preaching in the south in the countryside of Judea. One of my fondest memories of the start of this chapter in my life was when we traveled to the small village of Cana, which was just a little north of Sepphoris, for the marriage of my brother James to a wonderful girl from that village. Following the wedding, we moved to Capernaum, where the other followers were added to our group. Our small group had now expanded to sometimes over fifty people, and as we walked from village to village and town to town, larger numbers of people would come out and listen to my teaching. I, along with John, who was preaching to the north, would talk about the importance of sharing what we had with others, and I discussed the need for all of us to interpret the times in which we lived. I told people that we needed to be prepared for the end times of our lives, as surely the kingdom of God was upon us.

Those were exciting and stressful times for my people. Rabbis all over the land were talking about the prophesies of Daniel, and since that time was a Sabbatical year, which was seemingly ushering in a final seven-year period before the perceived Apocalypse (thought by many Jews to be a time of insightful learning and renewal), there were numerous *anointed ones*, preaching the end times and urging folks to change their ways and live different lives. Some felt that I too was anointed. The Greek word *apokalypsis* referred to the revealing of secrets, sometimes by a kind of teacher, who would provide revelations that might transform a society, kind of an end times in preparation for the new world that would follow. That was a key part of my message: Through love of God and by loving others, the world could be changed. The old world would end, and a new world would begin. Many people at the time perceived that John the Baptizer was the priestly messenger preparing the way for a person to lead the people. Since John was a teacher of the tribe of Levi and I was a teacher from the tribe of Judah, many people were enthralled by our messages. John's message of repentance was delivered with great zeal and earned him harsh retributions from the rulers of our lands. The councils of the Pharisees in Jerusalem were growing anxious over John's and my successes in our baptizing and teaching about repentance. While my crowds had grown even larger than John's, it became apparent that there was a growing opposition to John's harsher words, and eventually John was arrested, tried, and executed by Herod Antipas, ruler of Galilee and Perea. Herod Antipas had transferred the center of his power to the town of Tiberias, which was found on the western shore of the Sea of Galilee within a day's walking distance just south of Capernaum. John, never one to mince words, had denounced Herod for marrying Herodias, who had been the wife of his brother Philip, and Herod was under the perception that John was preparing a rebellion.

MY FIRST MINISTRY

With John's execution, the undercurrent of unrest in Judea seemed to ferment. When I learned of John's beheading, I walked to the town of Bethsaida on the north side of the Sea of Galilee, which was the hometown of my followers Peter, Andrew, and Philip. My followers and I sought refuge, and amid the surprise and grief over the death of John, I spent a lot of time praying and searching my soul for what I should do next. My attempt at seeking sanctuary was thwarted in that dozens and then hundreds of people, many of them being John the Baptizer's followers, traveled in an attempt to find us and ask for counsel. Many times, my closest friends and I had to board boats to try to escape the onslaught of masses of people, and so we tried to sail to find places at which we might dock to seek refuge. Once Bethsaida was discovered as our encampment, we journeyed north for three days to the town of Caesarea Philippi near an area called Panias. A man named Pontius Pilate had been appointed by the Roman emperor, Tiberius, as the military ruler of Judea. Pilate proceeded to prove that he was a ruthless tyrant, even to the point of taking money from the temple treasury to pay the costs of completing an aqueduct into Jerusalem. The unrest of the Jewish people under Pilate grew.

The Jews throughout Judea were in an uproar, and Pilate responded to several riots by killing many of the riot leaders and participants. I received word that Pilate was investigating my own ministry, and I grew fearful for the lives of my followers. I began to talk to my closest followers about what might be my own fate, which would surely include suffering, but they continually scoffed at the whole notion that an emerging leader or

Messiah, such as myself, would meet with such a fate since I had promised them that the kingdom of God was at hand and had foretold that twelve of my closest followers would occupy their own positions of power. I chastised them in conversation, especially Peter, for they simply refused to understand fully what I had been attempting to prepare them for regarding the future. As I preached with allegories and parables and spoke with metaphors, I attempted to tell stories that could be understood on many different levels. If these stories might be repeated by spies to Herod, then the deeper meanings would be lost in simply the surface stories. But I knew that Herod would not stop with the blood of John the Baptizer if he sensed that there still might be an undercurrent of insurrection among the Hebrew tribes.

I was called a rabbi by some, a messenger or a teacher by others, and some referred to me as "lord," *maryah* in Aramaic, or *adonnay* in Hebrew, which meant, among other things, an authoritative teacher. People who listened to my preaching and who engaged me in conversations and discussions sometimes called me Hasid, Messiah, or the Son of God, which meant that they thought of me as a devout man. Many others who were contemporaries of mine also roamed the Galilean countryside and were addressed the same as I was, such as the rabbi named Carabbas, whom I mentioned earlier, and the saintly prophet called the Son of God, Apollonius of Tyana, as well as other maryahs or adonnays, such as Pythagoras, Empedocles, Aristeas, Hermotimos, Epimenides, and Abaris. There were many traveling rabbis besides me named Jesus (a most common name of that place and time), such as Jesus, the brother of Onias; Jesus, the son of Phabet; Jesus, the son of Damneus; Jesus, the son of Gamaliel; and Jesus, the son of Josadek, among others. I was Jesus bar (son of) Josef from Galilee. There were many teachers who were called by the Greek term *christos* or *christ* (the anointed one)—Theudas Christ; Bar Kochba Christ; and Jesus Christ, the son of Sirach—all of whom lived in the same time as I did. Like these others, I too was called by some as Jesus the Christ.

I pointed out that a lot of the Psalms were about the righteous suffering at the hands of their fellows. I knew that I could not return to my hometown area, as this might put my friends in danger, so my group traveled back to the town of Cana, where the family of my brother's wife provided us with sanctuary. After spending several months in Cana, we eventually returned to Capernaum, and soon thereafter, throngs of people began to arrive to hear me preach. The tides were seemingly rising toward some kind of eventual confrontation among the Jewish leaders in Jerusalem, the Roman rulers, and me. I chose seventy representatives and divided them, as I had earlier done with the twelve, into two-person groups. I directed them to travel ahead of me to spread my good news, heal, and proclaim that the kingdom of God was near. I had taught these followers how to use their faith and skills to heal and to cast out the spiritual demons that had inflicted people. As time passed, many of these two-person teams returned very excited over what they were able to accomplish, but they said that Herod's advisors were observed infiltrating their meetings, and it appeared as though he was preparing a list of possible incriminations against me, similar to what he had done against John the Baptizer. I remember that I did not feel that the time was right for a confrontation, so I moved my entourage and group of followers, which had grown to several dozen, to the high country of Gilead to seek temporary sanctuary.

During the winter months, I slipped into Jerusalem during the Hanukah festival in an attempt to decipher the atmosphere among the people there but was discovered by the Jewish authorities as I was strolling in the Portico of Solomon at Herod's Temple, wherein they confronted me by demanding that I tell them once and for all whether or not I considered myself the Messiah. I replied cryptically to them that since they were not my sheep, they did not believe. This upset them to no end, and they became quite enraged. In the confusion that followed, I was able to escape back across the Jordan River to my followers, who were camped at Wadi Cherith. We stayed there throughout the winter months, but when spring arrived, I felt that it was finally time to confront the Jewish leadership in Jerusalem with my teachings.

MY MINISTRY

My preaching focused on the serene growth that is possible throughout a person's life, the planting of seeds through which come mature plants and a personal harvest bearing fruits. I taught mostly about how the kingdom of God which means fulfilling one's true potential in life, is not dependent upon material wealth and the accumulation of things, but even the poorest among us can become the richest in terms of morality and values. I taught that the current world is in imbalance, and those who are the most unfortunate will emerge the victors if they follow the moral compass of living a righteous life. In many ways, this angered many of the religious leaders of that time and place. It was my desire not so much to create a counterculture to the ruling society of the Pharisees, Sadducees, and the Roman rulers but to urge people to seek their own self-reliance and self-actualization with godly virtues at the center of their lives. I taught that human life and worth superseded the many rules and laws made by society. I taught that nobody knows when a son of man will bring about the end of a person's life, but everyone should be prepared every day. I taught that our world is not the most important reality; we are only surrounded by things. Owning things is unimportant. What is important is that we have come from God's light and that when we are born, we become two entities: body and soul. Our goal is to become one again with God's light, away from this material world.[13]

I taught that I was anointed by the Spirit of God and often preached that those who are the poorest are the most fortunate in the eyes of God, as are the hungry, the grief stricken, and also those who are hated by others because their plights will end with the most rewards, as they had the most to gain. I taught that within the realm of overall spirituality, a radical reversal in a society from the top to the bottom of a people's culture would occur. Many of my apprentices and the followers of my cousin John the Baptizer as well had begun to call us the two Messiahs, one of us was the "Davidic King" and the other the "Anointed Priest." I heard these comments but remained silent. I was content to be the messenger of my Father in heaven, the Lord God Almighty, and to spread the Good News to all who would listen. It was up to the hearts and minds of those who heard me to decide for themselves. I often spoke with confidence that I saw myself as an envoy of God, a "Son of God" if you will, a role transmitted to me by God through the Holy Spirit ascribed to me at my baptism by my cousin John. However, when my followers attempted to change my meaning, by calling me Messiah, and said that I would become king or usurp ruling powers, I refused to allow them to think of me in this context.[8]

My apprentices began to refer to my message as my way or "the Way." I taught that though your sins shall reach from earth to heaven and though they shall be redder than scarlet and blacker than sackcloth, if you turn to what is taught with all of your heart and call your God your Father, you will be harkened as a holy people. I taught my followers to resist the proud but give grace to the humble. And let us be humble, temperate, free from all whispering and detraction, and justified by our actions, not our words. We are not to be justified by ourselves—not our own wisdom, knowledge, piety, or the works that we have done—but by the faith in which God Almighty has justified all people from the beginning.

I also taught that every person has two angels (or moralities) with him or her at all times; one is righteousness, and the other is iniquity. They are in competition for the person's soul. When the angel of righteousness gets into your heart, you talk with modesty, chastity, bountifulness, forgiveness, charity, love, and piety. When the angel of iniquity gets into your heart, you become bitter, angry, foolish, anxious, fearful, prejudiced, and ambitious.

So how do people distinguish the wicked from the good? Only God can do this. Just like in the winter, you cannot tell the dead plant from the living, so too you cannot tell the wicked from the good. Some plants appear dry but are alive. Some people appear on the outside to be good and devout, but their souls are bad and evil. Likewise, some people appear to live wicked or evil lives, but their souls are righteous and good.

My basic way of teaching was in the form of storytelling and allegory. Stories, fables, and myths can be understood on not just one literary level. A story has a plot, characters, a place and time, and sometimes a start and then a middle followed by an ending or closure. But stories, when mused over, can have underlying messages, signifying a thing other than what was said. Scriptures possess a literal and historical meaning, but they also contain deeper dimensions. There are deeper mysteries, a living word that breathes through the scriptures, stories, and narratives. As time passed, I learned that my stories were told, retold, and repeated numerous times; sometimes these stories were embellished or exaggerated, but most of the time, the gist of the stories and my activities survived, albeit in various forms.[14]

I taught that there are basically two ways a person can live his or her life—one way of life and one way of death. If you choose the way of life, you will love God and you will love your neighbor as yourself. You will live your life organized around God and others. This process takes many years of learning within a community. The darker way of living a life focuses on death, evil, the instantaneous gratification of desire, and taking advantage of those less fortunate. I taught through allegory, and it takes a keen intellect to peel away the layered messages; the allegorist looks for the truth found behind the story. Seek God and seek the common good.

I taught that those who are the poorest in spirit can discover the best of life and can encounter the kingdom of heaven. I preached that those who mourn could be comforted. I said that the meekest among us could inherit the earth's blessings. My teachings centered on the notion that if people hunger and thirst after righteousness, then they can be filled. I taught that people reap what they sow; therefore, if you are merciful, then you will obtain mercy. I taught that it is important not to hide one's faith under a bushel but to display it to the world like the light of a candle for all to see. And when others view your faithfulness and observe your good works, this brings glory to God. I told people to provide alms and assistance to those who are in need but not to boast about what they give, not even keeping track themselves of the good they do so that their left hand figuratively is unaware of what the right hand is doing to help others. I taught that people's most important prayers are conversations between them and God, talks behind a door shut to others. I taught my followers not to pray repetitiously but forthrightly and boldly, for God our Father knows what things we need even before we ask. I taught that our most important possessions are never things but the treasures found within our own heart. I warned people not to judge others or to worry about their future but to spend their time being on the lookout for the daily evils with which they are confronted. I told my followers to be wary of false prophets and teachers and to look into the good treasure of the heart, which brings good deeds. I beseeched those who listened to me to unburden the yoke of that which they were heavily laden and taught that my teaching would give them rest, as my yoke was easy and my burden for them was light. Love God, and love each other.

I taught with parables. For example, I told a story about a sower who threw some of his seeds by the wayside, and fowls came and ate them up. This was a metaphor for those who perform good deeds, but because their intentions are not good, evil takes over. The sower who casts seeds upon stony places resulting in poorly growing plants, which have little soil to sustain growth, is likened to a person who hears the word of God but fails to joyfully act on what was taught because the roots of love have not grown deep within his or her soul. The sower who casts his or her seeds among thorns is like a person who cannot grow in goodness because of the deceitfulness of earthly riches, which choke the soul. But when the sower plants his or her seeds in good soil, it is like the person who hears the word and understands it; while acting out of love for God and others, that person will bear the fruit of humanness up to a hundredfold.

I once replied to the question, "When will the kingdom of God come?" The answer is whenever "two shall become one, and that which is without as that which is within; and the male with the female, neither male nor female." The deeper meaning here is that the kingdom of God is found when we speak the truth to each other without hypocrisy. Put another way, our anger is the male and our love for each other can be thought of as the female, both physical attraction and lust or agape love, sometimes called concupiscence. When these two are overridden by reason, then there is in us neither male nor female. I said that which is without as that which is within, meaning my teaching calls the soul that is within and the body that is without. Therefore, as your body appears, so let you be seen by its good works.

I spent three years roaming the Galilean countryside, urging followers to seriously think about how they worshipped, prayed, and lived their lives. I was a practicing Jew, but as the months passed into years, I grew to sense that my people were more concerned about the rituals and ceremonies of their faith than giving to their fellows. I understood that failing to uphold every law created a kind of humility in a person, which may be what the Jewish leaders desired, but I became worried that people were more concerned about the intricacies of blood sacrifices of animals in the temple than they were about sacrificing for each other. I preached that I did not intend to change the law of Moses one tiny bit but to encourage all people to simply love God and each other, and then the law would be upheld.

I became known not only as a rabbi and preacher but also as a healer. For example, sometimes relatives of the ill would come to me and ask me to perform miracles, such as asking me to regrow limbs that had been amputated or to destroy terrible infections, which were beyond my healing powers. But other times I was able to use my faith and wisdom to assist. One time, a synagogue ruler named Jairus pleaded with me to heal his daughter, who was near death. When I went to his home and inspected his ill twelve-year-old daughter, I told his family that she was past the worst of her affliction, and she quickly revived; all the while, the family celebrated her turn for the good. I told the family not to publicize their good fortune or to tell others that their daughter had been raised from the dead, as this would bring undue light on my ministry.[6]

Slowly, I came to realize that an overarching sacrifice was somehow going to be needed by myself to create a new covenant. As this notion evolved, the means of how this would happen entered my daily prayers. The underlying mystery of life, which I attempted to teach to my followers, is that God, the King of heaven, is in each of us, and conversely, we, as godly beings created by God, are part of God's kingdom. The kingdom of God is available in each one of us. Our old selves must die to be reborn anew within the kingdom of God. This wisdom that comes by discovering the kingdom of God within ourselves will allow us to always be one with God. This is the purest form of self-knowledge that might be understood.

Within the experience of the despair of life, a person needs to experience this wisdom, and all of that person's ignorance and anxiety will be dispelled. The message I tried to convey time and again was that the kingdom of heaven is within you, and whoever knows him- or herself shall find it. Put another way, the root of the message is to *know yourself*. The reality of what is around us as we live our lives is not really a thing at all. What matters is our conceiving, our world and that which witnesses the reality; it is our consciousness itself. Our essential identity is our awareness, our trust in God.

I told my closest followers that my message of love was too much for our small group to spread over a large area. If we were to stay together too much longer, the authorities in Jerusalem would grow more suspicious of our teaching. We were competing with many messianic leaders and their small groups who were roaming the countryside. Some of these leaders were teaching a violent overthrow of the Roman rule over our land; some were teaching about the end times when our people might perish at the end of our world. Others dared to preach about worshipping gods other than the God of Abraham and our people. I told my closest students and apprentices that should anything befall me, my family members, or other members of our group, they were charged to continue my message. I urged them to travel to the ends of the earth to teach and to heal the mental demons of depression, melancholy, and despair among all the people they might meet. I urged them to baptize followers to the Way, to love God, and to love others, as this would transform the world. We made a pact between us that we would teach our message as long as we lived.

In my many travels around the world, I had come to realize that God might be represented as a point. A point is a geometric concept that has no characteristics and no dimensions. This point in our lives is the one, the beautiful, and the truth; it is love. This point is to what we all aspire, as simple as unconditional love. The only way to travel toward this point is through repentance, not apologizing for the bad things we have done but enacting an actual change in our behavior, from the dissatisfaction with the way we have been and the purposeful desire to be different. In a way, that was the deeper meaning of baptism. We need to be purified and cleansed by examining our failings in order to become better. We need to rise from our old selves to become better humans.

DEATH

By the end of March, I felt that the time had arrived to both confront the leaders of the ruling Sadducees and to fulfill my destiny. Rumors continued to circulate that both the Jerusalem authorities and Herod were plotting to kill me, but still I forged ahead. By then, our small group had grown to a much larger entourage, swelled by both the curious and by my stalwart followers. Besides my closest compatriots, my mother and sisters, and the families of my students, a woman named Joanna, whose husband was one of Herod's household officials, and another named Susanna, along with Mary Magdalene, assisted our group with expenditures, purchasing food and supplies. People began to publicly shout, "Jesus, son of David, have mercy upon me!" which aroused great anxiety among the authorities that I was preaching rebellion as a messianic leader. I began to sense that in confronting the authorities, I might cause a dialogue to ensue between them and myself, which could synthesize the causes of our people and present a unified force against our Roman conquerors.

On a Sunday, once we reached the outskirts of Jerusalem at the small village of Bethany at the time of Passover celebrations, I elected to enter the city. The city was alive with the preparations for the Passover festivities, and my arrival seemed to be just one more event of interest to passersby, as they congregated to view us slowly walking along the streets. The people in the crowds yelled, "Hosanna to the Son of David!" among other slogans, and my friends grew afraid, asking me to deny any association with a messianic prophecy. I countered their fears by telling them that if I did ask the people to be silent, even the rocks along the streets would cry out the need for change. Later in the evening, we returned to Bethany where we were housed in the homes and dwellings of Mary and her sister Martha.

The next day, I walked to the temple. My message all along had centered on bolstering the plight of the economically poor and of the poor of spirit. A couple of days later, I encountered representatives from the temple, officials who confronted me publicly in attempts to get me to break openly with Roman law. One man yelled from a crowd, asking which of the Torah's commandments was the greatest of them all. I quoted the Jewish Shema as his answer, "Hear, O Israel, Y-hweh our God, Y-hweh is One, and you shall love Y-hweh your God with all your heart, and with all your soul, and with all your mind, and with all your strength," and said that the second was to love each other. The man continued our dialogue by responding that if a person loved God and loved others, then love would seem to be much more than all the offerings and sacrifices taking place in the temple. I responded to him that he was not far from the kingdom of God if he practiced that creed. Another man asked if I supported Roman taxation, which I immediately saw as a ploy to get me to publically refute Roman rule. I countered by saying that we should render to Caesar that which was Caesar's and give to God those things that belonged to God.

The next morning, Tuesday, Judas and I met. Judas was one of my most trusted friends and apprentices, and we discussed how best to go about initiating a confrontation with the top temple priests. My efforts to contact these men had been rebuffed earlier, and they were refusing my requests to discuss my teachings and my goals. My messages were evidently received by the assistants, who indicated that this meeting would not happen and that the priests and high officials were too busy with the Passover preparations. Judas and I agreed that something needed to be done to get their attention, and we made a plan to make them see me in person.[5] The temple laws seemed to state that if I were under arrest, they would be obliged to meet with me. We thought that if this could take place by that evening, then my confrontation with them might occur before the Sabbath on Friday. Judas agreed to go to the temple under the guise that he would turn me in to the authorities because of my perceived inflammatory teachings, and then they would have to talk with me when they met with me to examine my ideas and goals. I expected the temple priests to show up with the temple guards to escort me to the temple anterooms for our discussions, and once we were able to talk, they would see my sincerity and realize I did not mean to present a challenge to their power.

I asked my faithful followers to meet me at a house in the lower city of Jerusalem on Tuesday night, the thirteenth of the Jewish month of Nisan. We ate our meal, and I pleaded with them to understand the significance of our ministry and to pray for our success. I told them that I originally wanted to eat the Passover meal with them, but that this could not happen until I suffered what was about to happen and until the will of God was fulfilled. I knew that my meetings with the temple officials would be difficult and harsh, but I felt that the time had come. After sanctifying the food, I compelled my friends to consider my own flesh and blood as they consumed the bread and wine because I was the one who needed to take on the hostility and conversations of the temple priests. I asked them to eat and drink in remembrance of our message and me. James, my brother, was visibly shaken and seemed to understand that the kingdom of God was at hand, that our quest would soon be realized. James pledged that he too would not drink or eat until he witnessed the kingdom arrive through the temple authorities and I reaching an agreement.

I told Judas that he needed to do what he had been bidden, and he left, to the confused looks of others who were present. Judas did go to the priests and was successful in getting a meeting. He told them where I would be later on in the evening. Without his asking, the priests wanted to *reward* him for his information with a bag of silver coins. To maintain appearances, he took the money and proceeded to wait while they prepared to meet me.

When our meal was finished, I led my eleven remaining closest followers to a quiet olive grove called Gethsemane at the base of the Mount of Olives. We gathered at this place, which I knew well since I had used it as a place for solitude in the past. I asked my friends to sit and pray with me, but the wine and food took its toll, and soon they became drowsy and sleepy. As the night wore on, I grew agitated and worried. What if the priests did not come? What if they again refused to talk with me? What if they showed up with their entourage of assistants and temple guards? What if violence ensued and somebody got hurt? I worried that perhaps this confrontation had not been well planned and that too many pathways and options were up in the air, like leaves falling from trees without real direction.

Suddenly, in the late-night hours, I heard a huge commotion approaching us. I was heartened that Judas had succeeded and the temple priests were approaching. The sound increased in temper and loudness, as dozens and finally hundreds of men arrived. To my shock, not only were the priests and temple guards present, but a full detachment of Roman soldiers surrounded us. I was told that I was under arrest not by the temple authorities but under the orders of the Roman governor, Pontius Pilate. The priests had persuaded the governor that I posed a threat to the city's well-being. I would be taken to Pilate for a speedy trial. Matters happened too quickly for anybody to fully realize that I intended to be taken peacefully. Some of my friends reacted to my arrest with scuffling, and the soldiers who were present grew angry. In the middle of some fists being thrown by both groups and a lot of yelling and screaming, I was surrounded by soldiers and led off. My followers realized that resistance by that time would only be futile, and they managed to escape under cover of darkness into the night. As I was being taken away, I looked out of the corner of my eye and saw that Simon Peter and James were following us at a distance as we left the garden.

The events of the night and next morning became a blur to me, as the soldiers beat me, seemingly for hours. I was first taken to the house of a Sadducean priestly aristocrat by the name of Annas, who was the father-in-law to the politically appointed high priest Joseph Caiaphas. Annas was the real power among the Sadducees and had actually served as high priest himself in earlier times. Annas and five of his sons would all become high priests, and it was to this political dynasty my die had been cast. The full Sanhedrin council was not present, as this would have been over seventy individuals, some of whom were in good counsel with my teachings. Remember that my best friend, traveling companion, and uncle, Joseph, was in fact a member of the Sanhedrin. Annas's political power was so strong that he wielded a tight-knit group within the inner group of the Sanhedrin who had mustered together in the very early morning hours to put me on trial. I remained silent during most of their rants and accusations, but finally, worn out physically by the activities and beatings of the long night, I responded to them that I considered myself the messiah hoped for by our people and said that they would see the Son of Man sitting at the right hand of power and coming with the clouds of heaven.

I was confronting the priests the best way I knew how, by explaining to them that if they would not lead our people into a new way, then I would. I intended that our people would be given power, and we must change. Annas laughed at me and scoffed at the notion that I might muster a change in the power structure in Jerusalem. He told me that he had no interest in my teachings about love and care for the poorest among us but that he intended to destroy me. I realized at that moment how grossly I had underestimated his passion for power and came to the terrible realization that my plans had gone awry.

Many of my followers would blame the entire Jewish world for my death, but one of the most important reasons for my writing this narrative is to set the record straight. The Jews who knew me, who listened to me, and who talked to me were appreciative of my message and wanted no harm to come my way. I presented a new dialogue. I presented a different ideal for the world. No! It was Annas and his cohorts at the temple who should be blamed for my murder. It is easy to find scapegoats in an attempt to gain understanding of complex issues. Ultimately, this became quite a simple issue against me. The lust for power by one man and his colleagues was my downfall. As history has proved time and again, the influence of just one person, for the good or for the bad, can affect change.

But my fate continued in a downward spiral that morning. When the inner circle of the Sanhedrin voted me guilty and sentenced me to death,

I was taken outside and beaten mercilessly by the guards, on the orders of Annas. I was taken within hours to the royal palace buildings where Pilate was then residing. Annas charged me with political misdeeds, including being a threat to the Roman rulers. Governor Pilate seemed reluctant to grant the wishes of Annas. He had grown tired of the wandering rabbis, walking around the countryside claiming to be messiahs. Pilate seemed merely to want my situation to go away. He even said that he did not need this issue, my death, to complicate the Passover festivities being attended by the many thousands who were coming to Jerusalem that weekend. One of my secret followers, a man named Nicodemas, who was also a member of the Sanhedrin, was allowed to argue on my behalf, as was the custom at these kinds of hearings, but in the end, economically, these were the most important few days of the entire year for merchants in the city. A trial and death sentence of a messianic figure like me would only bring heightened stress to what was already a fragile relationship between the Roman authorities and Jerusalem's internal religious power structure, headed by Annas. Pilate needed to distance himself from my predicament.

Annas had arranged for a throng of his supporters to be mustered outside of Pilate's military offices outside the royal palace. Pilate took me outside and offered to the assembled mob to free me in accordance with the Roman custom of freeing a Jewish prisoner during our annual festival. The crowd, however, in a prearranged plan hatched by Annas and his followers, countered with a demand that Barabbas, another insurrectionist (who was secretly financed by Annas himself), be freed instead of me, urging instead that I be crucified. I became dazed and dumbfounded. I was astounded that this was happening. Pilate brought out a dish of water and symbolically washed his hands in front of the crowd, showing that he was not responsible for what was about to take place. Pilate learned from Annas that I was a Galilean and so, as one last attempt to remove himself as a cause of my death, ordered me to be taken to the quarters of Herod Antipas, the ruler of Galilee, who was nearby in Jerusalem for Passover.

Herod examined me for a short time but was wary of changing any decisions that had obviously already been concluded by Annas and his fellows. In the end, Herod knew that in Jerusalem, Royal Governor Pontius Pilate actually had political authority over such matters, and because the jurisdiction was with Pilate, he merely agreed with the sentence and ordered that I be returned to the governor to be killed as soon as that very day, before the Passover meal could be celebrated the next day.

I am thankful my memory of the ensuing hours on that Thursday became blurred by the numbness that engulfed me because of the pain and agony I suffered. If this had been the result of my plans, then I had no inclination or idea of what awaited me. I was taken from Pilate one last time to a courtyard outside the palace and stripped of my outer garments. I was flogged and beaten repeatedly by my Roman guards, as was the custom befitting political prisoners. My scourging was because I was found guilty of political crimes, not religious heresy. Through my tears, sweat, and blood, I saw blurred images of my skin being flayed from my body by the whips. I screamed and lost consciousness repeatedly. A wreath of thorns was implanted into my scalp. I could not see through the blood pouring into my eyes, and I grew dazed and fainted again and again. I screamed for all who could hear me that my suffering was for all who were poor, lost, and downtrodden. I tried to make sense of the event unfolding around me and attempted to find meaning. When I would briefly regain my senses, I yelled at those who were nearby witnessing my torture that it was my plight to carry the pain of their sin so that their souls might find peace. This would be the grace they sought. I caught glimpses of the faces of my family and friends in the mass of onlookers. Their sobs and tears gave me the strength to endure.

Finally, a patibulum or crossbeam for my crucifixion was tied to my shoulders, and I was led slowly to the outskirts of the city to my death. A sign was tied around my head, which read, "This is Yhoshua, King of the Jews," so that onlookers would have no doubt about why I was being sentenced to die—not as a religious leader or messiah but as a person who falsely claimed political power as king. This was one last attempt by the Roman authorities to distance themselves from the internal religious intrigues of Annas, my tormentor. This was to be a political execution, not a religious issue.

When I arrived at the place outside of the city called Golgotha, I was forced to lie on the patibulum, which had been untied from my body, while large nails were hammered into my forearms and into my heel bones, as my feet had been crossed over each other. I was feeling the unbearable pain from the scourging, and the pain of the nails piercing my skin, tendons, ligaments, and muscles was just one continuous blur. I was hoisted onto the cross. Two Zealots—other political prisoners—were crucified at the same time as I was. Their names were Gestas and Dimas. In my suffering, as I looked at their faces, I knew that I looked just as they did; a horrified look of humiliation, pain, anguish, and ghoulish ash was reflected back to me. I observed blood seeping out of their wounds, and I grew faint.

I remember hoping that my followers would realize that I was to die for the sake of love, to create a model of self-sacrificial passion for all people. Salvation could mean imitating me in my love for others, the love that God would reveal in my death for my friends. Human hearts could be atoned, creating a deeper love for God and transforming fear and hate to love. God becomes the great Mother who brings forth justice, redemption, and virtue with an orderly process of human and divine activity through a cosmic synergy or unity.

I wish that I could remember the words I said, but alas, I cannot. I have faint images of seeing my mother and my brother James gathered a distance away. I vaguely remember mumbling to one of my followers to care for our mother. I kept fainting and reawakening. There were less than a dozen onlookers. This was a Thursday morning, and everybody in the city was preparing for the Passover meal to begin the holiday celebrations the next day. Some political prisoners being crucified outside of the city was just too common an event to draw much of a crowd. I felt an overwhelming sense of failure at that moment. I had failed to impart my message to the ruling priests. I had failed my family and followers. And I felt that I had failed God. I vowed that somehow I should not have jeopardized the lives of my friends. I began to dream. I dreamed of the image of a dove ascending above my body, flying ever so quietly away from me into the sky. I remembered images of my childhood, of my father, of my childhood friends, and of the many places to which I had traveled. I dreamed of my followers as I taught them my message and tried to show them the Way, and I smiled. Slowly, ever so very slowly, I crept off to sleep, and finally, blackness overtook my senses and the pain stopped.

I died that afternoon. I had been on the cross for five hours. My pulse slowed, my heart stopped, and I lost consciousness. Later on, I was told that one of the guards grew upset that I expired seemingly so quickly, drove a spear into my side, and found only water seeping from that wound and not a gush of blood. If he had hit one of my vessels, it would surely have been blood seeping from that wound, but he did not. An officer present decided to order the guards to haul my body down, remove the nails, and wrap me in some cloth blankets.

AFTERMATH, THE MIRACLE, AND MY RESURRECTION

I was told later that my childhood companion and uncle, Joseph, had arranged with the authorities to take possession of my body. A group of his colleagues carried me to a roughly constructed sepulcher on some property on the outskirts of Jerusalem that he owned in what was known as the Garden of Joseph. I was placed on a hard rock slab. My wounds were cleaned, and I was washed thoroughly, as was the custom; then I was left alone as night fell over the countryside.

To myself and to those around me, I was dead. I was unconscious and not moving, and I am sure that my heart had stopped beating. I have only a foggy recollection of a series of nightmares and horrible visions that passed before my mind in the ensuing hours. I had a sense that I was in some kind of otherworld. I was in pain, and the people around me were in pain too. There was sobbing, crying, screaming, cries of agony, and visions of death, torture, and illness. I was in hell. I was visited by demons, monsters, fallen angels, and anguished people who felt betrayed and hated and were in horrible agony. I felt that I had a fever of unexplainable magnitude, and I myself felt pain and abandonment. I wondered if this was what was awaiting me after death, and then I became confused and sick. After a while, I again drifted off to a black nothingness. I had died.

The next day—actually, it was eventide—I slowly became aware of my body again. The pain of my wounds was still present, but miraculously, the sensations were bearable, and I slept for hours. I awakened to early morning. I felt rejuvenated, and my energy had returned. I prayed, and my Father God spoke to me, saying that I was his Son and that my return to life would have great meaning for our world. I was hungry and covered in dried sweat, and my wounds were starting to scab over. Joseph and one of his friends showed up at the tomb, and to say that they were surprised to discover that I was not only alive but was healing quickly is an understatement. They carried me out of the tomb,[9] and we went to his home, where I was given food and clothes, covered in blankets, and allowed to rest. When I arose from sleep the next day, we sat and talked for hours. Joseph told me that when the Sanhedrin inner circle discovered that he had taken possession of my body, guards had taken him prisoner by orders from Annas and Caiaphas, and he was thrown into a windowless chamber overnight to be tried for taking my body. The door to his chamber was sealed, but the next day, his family was able to purchase his freedom. Joseph told me that even with his release, he did not feel that it was safe to remain in Jerusalem for very long.

What now? My family and followers thought I was dead, and the authorities were keeping watch throughout the city for any sign of disturbances. I could show myself to my mother and ask that she keep my whereabouts secret, I could visit with my followers by calling a secret meeting and plan our next strategy, or I could attempt to remain out of sight and think, pray, and decide on my next course of action.

My recovery continued over the next several days,[11] and I grew stronger. Joseph told me that guards from both the Roman authorities and the Sanhedrin were asking questions related to the whereabouts of my body and also my family and my friends. Once the Passover's festivities were over, the thousands of visitors to the city would be traveling back to their homes. Joseph told me that my closest comrades had held a meeting and had decided to continue my mission by accepting my charge to them to go out into the world and spread the good news.

I met secretly with my family and some of my followers and urged them to continue spreading my ministry by teaching the precepts of my ideas and thoughts. The fact that I had risen after my crucifixion was highly affixed in their minds. I urged them not to preach in Jerusalem for a while since the authorities were bound to arrest them. I commissioned all of them to go forth, first to their own towns and then farther still, to preach about the Way. There was much crying and soul-searching, for we had been together, in one way or another, for three years or longer. But it was time to enact the next phase of our ministry, so we said our good-byes and farewells and wished each other safe journeys.

It broke my heart not to appear further to my family and followers, but to do so would have put their lives in immediate peril. My mission in Jerusalem seemed finished. What would be would be. I made an effort in the ensuing weeks to pass by the houses where, I had learned, some of my acquaintances were staying. Cloaked in new clothes purchased by Joseph, I walked the nearby streets. On several occasions, I passed within eyesight of people who knew me, and a few times, they appeared to look me in my eyes. I sensed a brief look of recognition on their faces. Joseph and his family swore to keep my whereabouts a secret, but stories began to circulate from people spotting me in a crowd or seeing me on a road. At times, I conversed with friends as we walked on surrounding roads in the countryside but felt that any actual continued contact on anybody's part would place their lives in jeopardy.

My time in Jerusalem was over. Over the next few weeks, I learned that my followers were dispersing throughout the surrounding areas. I learned that my followers, the sons of Zebedee, Thomas, Nathanael, Simon Peter, and a couple of others returned to the Sea of Galilee to again take up their fishing businesses, and I grew restless. The entire group of my family and followers had fled to the area of Galilee for safety, and I needed to depart as well.

MY CONTINUING MESSAGE

Joseph, who had provided me sanctuary, was restless as well. His family's merchant business was expanding, and he needed to consult with his business partners in other lands, as well as to search for new traders and reestablish his business and shipping routes. We conferred over this situation and decided that I might accompany him as he set sail on his next journey.

Setting sail to the far reaches of the Roman Empire, to Britannia, with my uncle Joseph was a multitier effort on my part.

First, after I had risen after my crucifixion, I knew that my continuing presence among my followers would have a twofold effect. If I were seen with them, then their safety would be in jeopardy since the Sanhedrin had arranged for my torture and execution and there was an undercurrent of fear directed against any of my followers. The movement we had generated was seen by the Jewish leaders in Jerusalem as part of an ongoing clandestine and covert rebellion against Roman tyranny in our lands, and many members of the Sanhedrin had political and economic ties to keeping the status quo. When one of my followers, Stephen, told an audience in Jerusalem that my teachings afforded me a seat on the right hand of God, the audience members grew violent, and Stephen was stoned to death. A growing number of traveling rabbis considered themselves part of the messianic prophecies, and many Zealots were openly advocating for civil war. I had clearly told my followers that I had not just taught my will but the will of God and that the will of humans and the will of God were not equal.[10] Even though I kept repeating this, it became apparent to me that as news of my preaching spread, adherents to my stories began to insist that I was the messiah of the Zealots, seeking a transformation of religious and political power as an equal of God. If I were to remain in the area of Jerusalem, then my followers would remain in danger. Secondly, I desired that my followers should disperse and traverse the land, preaching the Way of loving one's enemies, caring for others, and accepting the poor and downtrodden. If I were to remain among them, then my followers would tend to be reluctant to leave for other lands.

The second tier of my new effort was to personally travel to other lands to spread my message. Some of my earliest followers saw my message as being directed only to Jews—Simon Peter, for example. But as time passed, as my followers sailed to other lands and walked long distances spreading my word, Gentiles around the world began to enter into groups of my followers of the Way. Sailing with my uncle Joseph would afford me the guise of being a merchant trader and allow me easy access to foreign ports, giving me an opportunity to visit new places and talk to new peoples. I traveled to wondrously fascinating and culturally rich locations in Britannia, to far-off peoples west across the wide ocean, and to India. In Britannia, near the tin mines of Glastonbury, we started our first congregation.

I learned that regardless of culture, politics, or climate, people suffered the same problems as they lived their lives: illness, death, hunger, poverty, day-to-day hardships, weather, family conflict, war, rebellion, and politics. Religion and faith take many forms. People search for meaning in desperation, and humans attempt to understand the natural forces that impact them through literary inventions, myths, embellishments, and attributing human traits to astrological events. I taught that the basis of living together must center on love and understanding as well as caring for those individuals who are less fortunate. Every person is born in this world with positive physical and mental attributes as well as afflictions, both seen and unseen. Failing to help others as much as one can is to deny God in one's life.

As I continued to travel the world and time wore on, I learned of the fates of my most trusted followers. Bartholomew traveled to India,

THE AUTOBIOGRAPHY OF YHOSHUA BAR JOSEF THE ANOINTED

Ethiopia, Arabia Felix, Lycaonia, Persia, Parthia, the lands of the Medes, and finally to Armenia, where he was flayed alive and then beheaded at Albanopolis. James the Younger went to Syria to preach and returned to become the first bishop of Jerusalem, where he was martyred. John bar Zebedee preached in Ephesus, Patmos, and Rome and took care of my family, including my mother, after my crucifixion. Simon, my brother, sometimes called the Canaanite or the Zealot, preached in Egypt, Cyrene, Africa, Mauritania (he accompanied my cousin and me to Britannia), Libya, and Persia. He finally died with Jude as a martyr in Syria. Andrew (who traveled with Matthias) preached in Scythia and other lands in what is today called Russia (or Ukraine), parts of Africa, Thrace, Macedonia, Byzantium (founding churches along the way and ordaining the first bishop there named Stachys), Armenia, and Romania and was scourged and then hanged on a cross in the shape of an X at Patrae in Achia by the proconsul there, Aegeates. Matthew preached in Galilee and eventually went to Ethiopia, Persia, and then to Egypt, where he was martyred. Philip preached in Ethiopia in Africa, Scythia, Gaul (present-day France), and at Hierapolis in Phrygia, and he was martyred there, bound on a cross with his hands down and then stoned. Jude, my brother, went to Syria after my crucifixion and preached in northern Persia and Armenia as well. Thaddeus took my message to Armenia, Syria, and Persia. Matthias, who replaced Judas Iscariot in the inner circle of followers and was one of the seventy I sent out into the world, traveled to Macedonia and was tortured for his preaching in Ethiopia, but he was stoned to death in Jerusalem. James (the Elder) preached in Caesaraugusta (Spain), and he was martyred there. Simon Peter is best known for becoming a leader of followers of the Way. He traveled to Antioch, Corinth, Pontus, Bithynia, Cappadocia, Galatia, Britannia, Gaul, and Babylon and became the first bishop of Rome, where he was martyred by Nero. Thomas started groups of followers of the Way when I left Jerusalem by going to Syria, Perisa in the Parthian Empire, and provinces in the areas that would become Pakistan, Turkmenistan, Tajikistan, Edessa, Nisibis, and Malabar. He was speared to death as a martyr in Calamene, in India.

Within fifty years of my crucifixion, writings appeared that were attributed to various followers. An oral history, which began to be called Matthew, was adopted by a group of Ebionites, who came to be known as Jewish Christians. An oral history attributed to a Luke was adopted by followers of a leader named Marcion. Yet another oral history attributed to a Mark (which was the first to be written) was adopted by a group referred to as the Docetists, and a history attributed to John was adopted by early followers called Gnostics. Other histories and stories about my teaching also were passed around by various groups of followers, and some were copied and recopied, such as the letters of an evangelical follower named Paul, who started various groups.

With my relative John, I sailed to many lands, many of which had no names, across vast seas, and traveled over land. I learned that humankind everywhere has similar hopes and dreams, regardless of language or culture. All people have a divine spark within them and desire to return to God's light. My message can be compacted into five words: love God and each other.

POSTSCRIPTS

There is little mention of Jesus's birth stories until the third century.

In none of the earliest Christian texts are there any reports of Jesus appearing to his fol-lowers or disciples after his crucifixion. In the earliest of the Gospels, Mark, in the word-ing that first circulated in the first century CE, there is no mention of Jesus beyond His death. The final verse in the earliest scriptures in Mark appears to scholars to have been 16:8: "And they [the women] went out and fled from the tomb; for trembling and aston-ishment had come upon them; and they said nothing to anyone, for they were afraid." Over 250 years after the first mention of the book of Mark appeared, there suddenly was circulated another ending: what we know today as verses 9–20. The earliest Christian writers in the third century CE did not seem aware at all of this "extended version" of Mark, which appears to be written in Greek, as a very confusing rendition of what was appearing in the later written Gospels of Matthew and Luke. John appears to have appeared still later and expanded upon the previous three books.

The text of this autobiographical narrative clearly states that Jesus and His followers believed that he died and rose from the dead.

Beyond the New Testament stories, it is believed by many that Jesus died in Kashmir at an old age. The cultural historians there identify the holy man Yuz Asaf buried at the Roza Bal shrine in Srinagar, India, as Jesus on the basis of an account in the *History of Kashmir* by the Sufi poet Khwaja Muhammad Azam Didamari (1747) that the holy man Yuz Asaf buried there was a prophet and a foreign prince. It is important to understand the importance of belief and faith, though. The human spirit and intellect create myths and stories by which we can explain the complexities of reality and existence. History, eyewitness accounts, and collective memories based on oral traditions are complex interpretations and understandings. We know is that change is inevitable when it comes to "facts."

Many passages from the New Testament have been added since the first century, such as Jesus appearing before five hundred people at one time after his crucifixion. (Something this monumental would have resulted in multiple independent narratives existing at that time, but none exist.) Another scripture added much later was Matthew 16:18 when Jesus tells Peter, "Upon this rock I will build my church." This would have been very perplex-ing to Peter because the word "church" would not be invented until hundreds of years later. Jesus was a Jew, and he attended and presided over Jewish worship services his whole life. Jesus did not start a new church. These edits of the canon, however, do not detract from the original teaching of Jesus, in the opinion of this writer.

It might be noted that the first century CE was one of the best documented eras of history, and given this, there were no governmental or legal documentations of Jesus or his trial, execution, or appearance as a resurrected person. There were, however, various accounts of his death written in several non-canon works. The narrative herein is an attempt to synthesize these ideas.

There is no Roman record of a census being taken until the reign of the emperor Vespasian in 74 CE.

There is no historical evidence that a massacre of every infant boy in an area just six miles from Jerusalem in the time period of Jesus's birth occurred in any Jewish, Greek, or Roman documents. It is only found in the book attributed to Matthew.

It is noteworthy to mention that the most famous historian of this period never mentioned Jesus. Nicolaus of Damascus lived in the last of the first century BCE and died in the early first century CE. He was a tutor to Cleopatra and Mark Antony and friend, advisor, and court historian to King Herod the Great. He wrote a 144-book history of the world through the end of Herod's reign, relying mostly on Herod's personal memoirs and his own firsthand knowledge. Josephus cites Nicolaus as the major source for his own account of Herod's reign.

As a Christian, I enter the aforementioned narrative as an act of faith. It is not meant to be definitive nor is it presented as true.

ENDNOTES

Endnote 1 - The earliest Christian writings say that Joseph was a "tectonic," which covers a wide range of skills, not limited to carpentry but usually meaning a builder or master craftsman (including many aspects of trades such as blacksmithing, stone, and brick masonry and the creative arts.).

Endnote 2 - Jesus's sisters are named in several of the "lost Gospels" (including *Protoevangelium of James* 19:3–20:4 and the *Gospel of Philip* 59:6–11). Jesus's brothers are well documented in the New Testament canon, including Mark 6:3. Most scholars feel that these men are Jesus's real brothers, not cousins or half-brothers. James is sometimes referred to as "James the Lesser" or "The Just" who became the leader of the Christian church as the bishop of Jerusalem (Acts 12:17 and 15:13) after Jesus's crucifixion, and he is the top leader who presided at the Apostolic Council of Jerusalem. Paul called James the true brother of Jesus (Gal 1:18–19), and the writer of the epistle of Jude identifies himself as the "brother of James" (Jude 1). Three hundred years later the bishop of Rome would gather enough political power to emerge as the foremost bishop, and up until the start of the third century CE, the bishop of Jerusalem had equal power with other bishops.

Endnote 3 - Malachi 3:1 and later on in Malachi 4 the scripture intimates that God would send a prophet (Elijah) before the "day of the Lord." This can be ascertained also from Matthew 17:10–13.

Endnote 4 - James, today, is the patron saint of Spain, and legend has it that upon his death (recorded in the New Testament), his remains were relocated in Santiago de Compostela. Many pilgrims to this site wear the symbol of the scallop shell, which is traditionally an emblem associated with James.

Endnote 5 - The relationship of Judas to Jesus is a matter of historical interpretation and faith. If Jesus felt forewarned in dreams, revelations (the term "revelation" is translated from the original script, which originally meant "hallucination"), and premonitions that he needed to create an eventful action during the Passover celebration while in Jerusalem, he would go to one of his most trusted followers (Judas, for example, served as Jesus's group's "treasurer" and scribe) to help carry out his plan. The Gospel of Judas, discovered in the 1970s near the town of Beni Masah in Egypt, which was finally written down as a third-century document, provides accounts that were previously written that were attributed to Judas in the first century. The Gospel of Judas did not match the accounts of the last days of Jesus as created by the bishops after the Council of Nicaea, and it was ordered destroyed as unorthodox. Only until its rediscovery and translation did this document fill in some gaps that had been missing in the story of Jesus.

Endnote 6 - Mark 5:40–43

Endnote 7 - A note about time, calendars, and the life events of Jesus: It takes painstakingly involved study to correlate Old and New Testament scripture to historical events and then to transpose these dates into both the Hebrew calendar used in Jesus's time and the Julian (Revised) calendar used today. BCE refers to "before the current era," and CE refers to "current era." So, John the Baptist was born on 1 Nisan 3758, which was Sunday, March 17, 3 BCE. Note: John's father, the priest Zechariah, served in the eighth (eight-day) course of Abijah, which started on the weekly Sabbath of 7 Sivan 3757, which was June 2, 4 BCE. The archangel Gabriel reportedly appeared to Zechariah after 9:00 a.m. that same morning (Luke 1:5–25). Pentecost was "fully come" 9 Sivan (Acts 2:1), but various sects of the priesthood observed this earlier. Jesus was conceived on the first day of the sixth month of Elisabeth's pregnancy with John (Luke 1:36). Normal gestation to full term is 266–70 days, so if Jesus and John were both carried an average term of 267 days, then John was conceived about 28 Sivan 3757, which was Saturday, June 23, 4 BCE, placing Jesus's conception in Mary by the Holy Spirit exactly five Hebrew calendar months plus one day (148 days) later, on 28 Cheshvan 3758, which was Sunday, November 18, 4 BCE. Note that procreation was permitted on the weekly Sabbath (Gen. 1:27–28). Jesus would have been born before sunrise 1 Elul 3758, which was Monday, August 12, 3 BCE.

The wise men (magi) saw Jesus's star rising in the east, thus their own witness to this conjunction near the "king star" Regulus was judicially construed as Jesus's true date and approximate time of birth, 4:00 a.m. JST. Jesus was visited by the magi on the eve of 16 Tammuz 3759 (Matt. 2:1–12), which was Tuesday evening, June 17, 2 BCE. Jesus was ten and a half months old at the time. Note: This near-perfect Jupiter-Venus conjunction in Leo was six arcseconds from concentricity. When Venus is sufficiently elongated from the sun and the sky is crystal clear, Venus can barely be seen with the naked eye in broad daylight. This dazzling conjunction was significantly brighter than Venus was alone; thus, it was certainly visible in broad daylight in a clear sky—and we know that the sky was clear by the magi's own testimony! Extant historical and astronomical evidences have further proven incontrovertibly that Herod "the Great" died within three weeks after the "blood-red" total lunar eclipse of Saturday, January 10, 1 BCE. John the Baptist's thirtieth birthday was 1 Nisan 3787, which was Thursday, March 27, 27 CE, when "the word of God came unto John [the Baptist]" (Luke 3:1–23). Note: This date was exactly 483 true Hebrew calendar years after the date that Ezra left Babylon with Artaxerxes's decree to restore Levitical rule and the people to Jerusalem. This included the restoration of government and taxation and also "set up the walls thereof, and joined the foundations" (Ezra 4:12). No other kingly decree satisfies this literal, true Hebrew calendric chronology. John's preaching is told by all four Gospels; John the Baptist is sometimes known as the Elijah of prophecy. Jesus's thirtieth birthday was 1 Elul 3787, which was Friday, August 22, 27 CE. Note: At age thirty, Jesus became eligible for priesthood and temple service. This is why John the Baptist asked of Jesus, "I have need to be baptized of thee, and comest thou to me?" (Matt. 3:14). One lunation later, that is, one calendar month later, 1 Tishri 3788, was exactly 483 true Hebrew calendar years after the date that Ezra observed his first Rosh Hashanah (1 Tishri, Day of Trumpets, "New Year's Day") in Jerusalem, but more importantly, that prior year of 3304 (458–457 BCE) was a Jubilee Year (Lev. 25:9–17ff), so the new year of 1 Tishri 3305 (September 21, 457 BCE) started Daniel's forty-nine-year countdown to the next Jubilee, which was 3354, clearly emphasizing the atonement in Jesus's teachings. Jesus was baptized by his cousin John at the river Jordan on 1 Tishri 3788, which was Saturday, September 20, 27 CE. At one with God (John 10:30), Jesus commenced His divine ministry, "confirming the covenant with many" (Dan. 9:27). Note: The seventieth and final week of Daniel's prophecy commenced with the preaching of John the Baptist and with the ministry of Jesus. Just as the Hebrew day is counted by "evening and morning," divided by the Earth's rotation with respect to the sun, the Hebrew year is similarly divided by the spring and fall equinoxes, with a "1:1" correspondence of holy days: 1 Nisan (new moon)/1 Tishri (Rosh Hashanah), 10 Nisan (lamb selected)/10 Tishri (atonement), Feast of Unleavened Bread (15–21 Nisan)/Tabernacles (1–21 Tishri), and so on. Gabriel's conspicuous "dual emphasis" on John and Jesus was best answered by John himself when Jesus was baptized: "This is he of whom I said, after me cometh a man which is preferred before me: for he was before me. And I knew him not: but that he should be made manifest to Israel, therefore am I come baptizing with water" (John 1:30–31). And Jesus's own words: "Before Abraham was, I AM" (John 8:58). "I AM the root and the offspring of David the bright and morning star" (Rev. 22:16). The prophesied Messiah of the old-covenant scriptures (TaNaKh) was made flesh in Jesus. Jesus rode into Jerusalem on 10 Nisan 3791, which was Saturday, April 21, 31 CE. Note: This "Palm Sunday" (Zech. 9:9) was 187 calendar weeks (three and a half calendar years) after His baptism. Jesus was crucified at 9:00 a.m. on the Passover, 14 Nisan 3791 (Mark 15:25), which was Wednesday, April 25, 31 CE; suffering unimaginable pain, Jesus died shortly after 3:00 p.m. that dark afternoon (Matt. 27:45–50; Mark 15:33–37; Luke 23:44–46). Note: "Messiah the Prince" had been "cut off" literally in the "midst of the week" (Wednesday), in the midst of the seventieth Sabbatical year (Dan. 9:24–27), just as the prophecy had foretold 568 years before in ancient Babylon (Dan. 9:1ff). Jesus's body was taken down from the cross near sunset and was entombed after sunset on the eve of the high Sabbath of the Feast of Unleavened Bread (Matt. 27:57; Mark 15:42; Luke 23:54; John 19:42. The paschal lamb, the one "without blemish, a male of the first year," was selected on 10 Nisan (Exod. 12). This was the Passover meal (pesah proper) Jesus shared with His disciples on the eve of His crucifixion. The second pascha, the afternoon (hagigah) sacrifice, was starting at the time Jesus died, from three to five that afternoon. Jesus was God's lamb for both Passover offerings, and His sacrifice left all others of no effect. Jesus had literally become the Passover, the chosen lamb of God (John 1:29, 36). The destruction of the temple on 15 Av 3830, which was August 10, 70 CE—not the faulty "9 Av" of Talmudic tradition—fulfilled "he shall cause the sacrifice and the oblation to cease" (Dan. 9:27). This divine cause was Jesus's crucifixion nearly forty years prior to that date. Jesus rose three days and three nights (i.e., Thursday, Friday, Saturday) (Matt. 12:40) after His body was entombed, which would have to have been Saturday evening, April 28, 31 CE, counted as Sunday, the *first day* of the Hebrew calendar week (Matt. 28:1; Mark 16:2, 9; Luke 24:1; John 20:1, 19]. His resurrection was discovered at sunrise (5:00 a.m.) Sunday morning. Note: covered by a swath cloth and then wrapped in linen. His body was sealed in a nearby, newly hewn stone sepulcher of the disciple Joseph of Arimathea (Matt. 27:57–60). Joseph, Nicodemus, Mary Magdalene, and Mary mother of Jesus prepared and wrapped Jesus's body, arranging flowers and preparing spices according to the ancient custom as time permitted. These flower arrangements were not at first completed that fearful evening of 15 Nisan but were completed on Friday following the high Sabbath, with the final spices and ointments to be applied early Sunday morning. But of course, that final preparation was not to be; Jesus had arisen. Jesus the Nazarene was 11,944 days of age at His crucifixion. (Written and published by Ma'aminei YHSH ha-Notsri, 1999, no rights reserved, presented free to the public domain. Wikipedia) Most Christians simply do not think logically if they believe that Jesus was crucified on a Friday and arose on a Sunday—that is only two days later. Jesus was crucified on the Passover eve, on Thursday. He came out of his grave three days later—Friday, Saturday, and finally Sunday—and the open grave was discovered early in the morning on Sunday.

Endnote 8 - John 6:15

Endnote 9 - Gospel of Peter (verses 37–39)

Endnote 10 - John 6:38

Endnote 11 - Hosea 6:2 In the Greek translation, this scripture states that the Lord shall make us healthy following two days, and on the third day, we will rise and live with God. In ancient Judaism, this passage is used to focus on the resurrection of our spirits. We sin and must be reconciled.

Endnote 12 - A village called Nazareth did not exist in this part of the world at this time, and there is no Roman or ancient Jewish geographical account of this name on any maps, correspondence, or documents until much later. Many people confuse the term "Nazarene" as a person who is from some place much as someone might be referred to as a "Canadian." But in the first century CE, a Nazarene referred to a person who was in a sect or cult and not from a place.

Endnote 13 - The Gospel of Thomas, Saying 11

Endnote 14 - See the book *Jesus Before the Gospels* by Bart Ehrman.

Endnote 15 - 1 Corinthians 9:5

SMALL GROUP DISCUSSION QUESTIONS

Have you ever played a game of "gossip" or "telephone" and been amused at how quickly a repeated story can change, become embellished, and be exaggerated with each retelling? Soon, in the course of the people retelling the story, omissions, commissions, additions, deletions, and changes occur. Oral history can be a holy experience in many illiterate cultures, but details become lost and modifications happen, not with purpose but merely with time. Much has been made by Christian detractors about the lack of historical evidence pertaining to the events of Jesus's life apart from biblical canon. But faith and belief are amazing aspects of human existence. How is your belief and faith strengthened or weakened by this book?

Is it important to dwell on the gist or major tenets of a religion rather than trivia, minutiae, or details? Why?

The author of this book began with the assumption that Jesus lived and died and that through a physical and metaphysical miracle, he was reborn. How do you reconcile this premise with your own understanding of reality, theology, and experience?

Do you agree with the author in his summation that Christian belief can be boiled down to five words (love God and love others)? Is this too simple? Why?

Do you agree with the author in his presentation of a Christianity chronology that extends hundreds of years before Jesus lived in the first century CE and the history related to understanding Jesus that extends hundreds of years after his time on earth? Why?

Is there a compromise or synergy between conservative Christians and progressive Christians? Is there room for intradenominational religious debate? Is there room for interdenominational debate?

The author attempted to account for historical documentation that Jesus visited many lands around the world such as England and India and even the belief that He visited the new world. This remains controversial, even in light of many oral histories. Would your Christian belief be diminished or strengthened if incontrovertible proof of His postresurrection travels existed? Why?

Do you agree or disagree with the author's account of Jesus's "lost" years as a child, youth, and young man? Based on what you know and what your experiences are, how would your account differ?

Many thinkers have attempted throughout the ages to personalize the accounts and teachings of Jesus to be accessible in their own lives, from Thomas Jefferson, who "rewrote" his own New Testament, to professors of divinity. Is this even worthwhile in your own theology? Or is this somehow a form of heresy?

John Wesley, the founder of Methodism, wrote that Christians needed to use reason, experience, knowledge, and scripture to derive their own personal faith. In what ways do you do this?

A CHRONOLOGY OF BELIEFS AND HISTORIES RELATIVE TO CHRISTIANITY

BCE stands for "before the current era," which many students recognize as the old BC.

CE stands for the "current era," which many students recognize as the old AD.

> Thirtieth century BCE: Egyptian priests record the faith history of Horus, called the Son of God; born of a virgin mother (Isis); associated with the miracle of seven loaves; purified his soul with a baptism; followers practiced communion (with bread = flesh, wine = blood); and who cured the blind.
>
> Seventeenth century BCE: Babylonian priests record the faith history of Marduk, Son of God, who created the first man called Atum (appropriated by the Hebrews as Adam); followers practiced communion in worshipping the god Marduk.
>
> Thirteenth century BCE: Canaanite priests teach that God created the first human, named Lilith, who disobeyed God in her freethinking (much of the lower status of women among Jewish rabbinical teaching comes from this myth).
>
> Twelfth century BCE: Canaanite priests record the faith history of many gods, including the "most high" God Almighty

named El Shaddai, a precursor to a one-god Jehovah precept for Hebrew tribes (Gen. 17:1).

1305 BCE: Pharaoh Ikhnaton sets Aton up as the first monotheistic god in Egypt.

1200 BCE: The first mention of a small nomadic tribe called the Israelites appears in any written text that has survived.

Ninth century BCE: Hebrews borrow rituals, laws, and beliefs from Egyptian and Babylonian stories to create the Tanakh, incorporating such ideas as monotheism, an antipork diet, and prophesied messiahs as well as resurrection of the dead.

Sixth century BCE: Worship of Mithras is widespread throughout Asia Minor. Mithras is called the Son of God by his followers; born on the winter solstice (December 25) of a virgin mother; birth witnessed by shepherds offering gifts; had twelve disciples; and promised his followers that they would have eternal life. The sentence "He who will not eat of my body and drink of my blood, so that he will be made one with me and I with him, the same shall not know salvation" is found first in the book of Mithras.

539 BCE: Upon their return from exile in Babylon, Jews in Jerusalem rebuild the temple, starting a Second Temple Period.

521 BCE: Buddha preaches, and some ideas are incorporated into Hebrew religion. The Golden Age is at its zenith for worldwide religions, philosophy, and learning with Confucius, Zoroaster, Lao-tse, the Jewish prophets, and the Greek poets all of which add to Hebrew culture, and they are later incorporated into Christian culture.

450 BCE: The Torah becomes the moral compass for most Hebrew tribes.

400 BCE: The Five Books of Moses (the Pentateuch) take solid form.

Third century BCE: Around 200–255 BCE, seventy-two men translate the Tanakh into Greek, thus creating the Septuagint (sept

= seventy), which become the official basis of the Old Testament. Prior to this date, there was no official Jewish holy document.

165 BCE: The Book of Daniel is written; Judas Maccabaeus rededicates the temple in Jerusalem.

112 BCE: Rise of the Pharisees and Sadducees in Palestine; writing of the First book of Maccabees in Hebrew.

63 BCE: Pompey the Great destroys Jewish independence and Israel, and Judah falls under Roman rule.

47 BCE: The Roman army destroys and burns the largest library in the world at Alexandria, demolishing original (and only) copies of many works of antiquity. What books that could be reclaimed were moved to a neighboring Egyptian city (Serapeum) and later back to Alexandria in a newly built library.

37 BCE: Following the Battle of Parthia, Herod "the Great" is appointed as an independent ruler under Roman auspices.

31 BCE: After years of war, Octavian, nephew of Julius Caesar, restores order to the Mediterranean world.

12 BCE: Birth of Mary, mother of Jesus.

Before 4 BCE–after 6 CE: The New Testament says that Jesus had to be born before 4 BCE for Herod to be king of Israel (as Herod died in 4 BCE) (see Matt. 2:1) and after 6 CE when Quirinius became governor of Syria (see Luke 2:1–7). So Jesus's birth year is in question historically. Both scriptures cannot be correct.

3 BCE: Apollonius Tyaneus (d 97 CE) is born. He was considered by many scholars to have been the greatest religious figure of his time—famous throughout the Roman Empire, traveled throughout Syria, Israel, Egypt, Turkey, Greece, and India. According to the historian Philostratus and a dozen other chroniclers and writers of the time, Apollonius had a divine birth, practiced celibacy, cured the ill and blind, cleansed entire cities of the plague, could foretell the future, spoke to and fed the masses, was worshiped as a god, raised the dead, and was called the Son of God (entered herein just to show that there were other holy men roaming the countryside in Jesus's lifetime).

THE AUTOBIOGRAPHY OF YHOSHUA BAR JOSEF THE ANOINTED

6 CE: Galilee remains under the rule of Herod Antipas, a son of Herod "the Great," and Judea becomes a Roman province with its capital at Caesarea with day-to-day rule delegated to Caiaphas, the Jewish high priest.

14 CE: Tiberius becomes emperor of the Roman Empire, ruling until 37 CE.

8–18 CE: Most early oral narratives (winding up in the Gospels) of Jesus's life state that at the age of twelve, he impressed the rabbinical teachers at the Jerusalem temple with his knowledge and wisdom. (If we can place Jesus's birth either before 4 BCE or after 6 CE, then this would be the window of opportunity for this event to have happened.)

26 CE: Pontius Pilate is appointed as the prefect of Judea.

27–33 CE: Jesus begins his ministry (traditional dates).

29–36 CE: Jesus is crucified. There is a peculiar scripture in John 8:56: "The Jews therefore said to him: Thou art not yet fifty years old." Why would people have said that Jesus was not yet fifty if he was, say, thirty-three years old? Some of the earliest Christian writing stated that Jesus was in his forties when he was crucified, so if that is the case, then he was crucified between 45 and 55 CE, which really messes up the timeline of Jesus's life.

Jewish and Roman custom dictated that only a dead person's family member might receive a dead body once an execution took place, so if Jesus's body was given to Joseph of Arimathea, then he would have been a relative of Jesus. An uncle seems to be the most plausible.

34 (approximately) CE: Saul of Tarsus has visions (translated from the Greek word for hallucinations) of Jesus. Saul was a Roman citizen who had persecuted, tortured, and killed members of the new sect of Jews who were followers of Jesus's teachings. Following his visions, he changed his name to Paul and began a lifelong quest to spread the new Christian religion beyond Jewish culture to Gentiles throughout the Roman Empire. Paul was very educated and devoted.

37–38 CE: Paul's first visit to Jerusalem to visit with various Christian apostles.

41 CE: James, Jesus's brother, is entrenched as the first presbyter or bishop of Jerusalem.

43 CE: Peter arrives in Rome to begin his teachings among the Jews who live there.

44 CE: James (the Greater, the son of Zebedee) is executed in Jerusalem by Herod Agrippa I.

44–49 CE: Peter is preaching in Babylon.

48 CE: Paul's second trip to Jerusalem. This was the probable writing of his letter to the loosely organized Christian community in Galatia; Paul wrote in his messages that he only knew two things about Jesus: that He was crucified and that He had a brother and mother. Paul never mentioned Jesus's virgin birth, Jesus's father, life events, ministry, miracles, apostles, betrayal, or trial, and he knew neither where nor when Jesus lived or died. Paul seemed to consider the crucifixion spiritual, not physical, as he wrote, "I am crucified with Christ" (Gal. 2:19–20). He seemed to acknowledge that people may claim "another Jesus" (2 Cor. 11:4), and wrote that Jesus was perhaps not a human man but simply a "spirit" of God's Son (Gal. 4:6–14). These are all interpretations, however.

50 CE: Emperor Claudius expels Jews from Rome because "they were being agitated by the prompting of Chrestos."

52 CE: Peter arrives in Cranganore, India, (with his wife) in search of Christian communities established by members of the seventy apostles sent out by Jesus to spread the Good News of his preaching.

55 CE: Letters to the Corinthians from Paul first appear, as do the letters to the communities in Philippa, Thessalonica, and Rome.

57 CE: Paul addresses communities of Christians in Rome and makes his final trip to Jerusalem at the Apostolic Council of Jerusalem, in which he meets with James the Lesser—Jesus's

brother (bishop of Jerusalem)—and other disciples and apostles, the outcome of which was a compromise to extend Christian teachings to non-Jews. Some of the apostles remained in disagreement that the movement should be extended to non-Jews.

58 CE: The first stories from eyewitness accounts and oral narratives of the life of Jesus are written down—sometimes called the Q-document (lost to antiquity).

62 CE: James, bishop of Jerusalem and brother to Jesus, is martyred.

64 CE: Nero first persecutes members of the new Christian sect.

The first imprisonment of Paul in Rome.

64–66 CE: The first writing of the Book of Acts; Paul's martyrdom in Rome.

66 CE: Outbreak of a Jewish revolt in Judea.

67 CE: Peter is executed in Rome in Nero's circus.

69 CE: Linus becomes the second bishop of Rome; Andrew the disciple is martyred in Patras.

70 CE: The destruction of the temple in Jerusalem following a Jewish uprising.

73 CE: The Jewish Wars end. Jerusalem had been destroyed by the Romans and the temple sacked, and the Jewish diaspora began (truly, the end of the world for Jews as foretold in the Old Testament and discussed by Zealots).

Disputes arose between Jewish scholars and some followers of the Christian sect over the idea of monotheism; the Jews stated that there is only one true God, and some of the Christians stated that Jesus was also divine, thus making two gods, while some Christians stated that the Holy Spirit was yet a third god.

80 CE: The "book" called Mark begins to circulate among some Christian communities. Mark was probably first in existence as oral memory as early as 65 CE.

88 CE: Clement becomes the third bishop of Rome.

90 CE: *The Homilies of Clement* (a series of twenty sermons sent to Christians in Jerusalem), which addressed the controversies with the "messiah" Simon Magus.

95 CE: The "book" eventually called Matthew begins to circulate among some Christian communities (this is the first narrative to mention the virgin birth of Jesus).

The text titled *First Clement* is written, which is the first document to address the topic of "apostolic succession," which states that the leaders of the Christian churches (bishops) were to be considered successors of Jesus's disciples and their authority was to be followed. This doctrine of apostolic succession was a direct result of the failure of Jesus to return in the lifetimes of the people who knew him; people were becoming disenchanted with the Christian sect, and the movement needed some organized leadership.

96 CE: *The Didache* first appears and is the first discussion of early Christian ritual, which gives instructions for baptizing, fasting, praying the Lord's Prayer, and celebrating the Eucharist. This manual of sorts laid down the basic tenets of what it meant to be a follower of Jesus's teachings and formalized the process of entering into membership in a Christian community, dictating a long process (sometimes years) before baptism could be granted to a novice member.

Clement's First Epistle to the Corinthians addresses intra-church factionalism.

97 CE: The "book" eventually called Luke begins to circulate among some Christian communities. The books of Mark, Matthew, and Luke are sometimes referred to as the synoptic Gospels (seeing with one eye) as they shared many of the same sources and have much in common with the Q-document.

98 CE: The death of Peter's daughter, Petronella, in Rome.

100 CE: The "book" eventually called John begins to circulate among some Christian communities. John especially is written as a book for Gentiles and focuses on the divinity of Jesus.

101 CE: The Gospel of Peter circulates among early Christian groups but is later declared heretical by church leaders in the third century (recounting many biblical stories found in Matthew but including a fantastical account of Jesus emerging from the tomb as a giant supported by two enormous angels and followed by a talking cross).

105 CE: The book titled *The Wisdom of Jesus Christ* is first circulated among early Christian groups. It was a Gnostic interpretation of Jesus's teachings to his disciples following his crucifixion and involved an esoteric understanding of human existence. It was banned by Constantine but rediscovered as part of the Nag Hammadi library in 1947 and 1960.

109 CE: *The Apocalypse of Peter* is first circulated among early Christian groups, considered canonical by most proto-orthodox Christian groups, which describes the "end of days" scenario at the return of Jesus to reality on earth. But this work was eventually rejected for inclusion in the New Testament at the Council of Nicaea.

110 CE: Ignatius, the bishop of Antioch in Syria, is arrested and sent to Rome, and he writes letters urging Christians to follow their bishops.

112 CE: *The Apocalypse of Paul* is first circulated among early Christian groups, which reveals what life is like for Christian souls following death.

This is the date that Pliny the Younger, governor of the Roman province of Bithynia, wrote a letter to Emperor Trajan for advice on how to deal with a group of accused cultists who had been brought into his court. This letter is the first recorded instance of Romans recognizing Christianity as a new religion.

114 CE: Emperor Trajan approves the executions of Christians for refusing to worship Trajan's cultic image.

125 CE: The first historical mention of the word "Christian." "Christians…a class of men given to a new and mischievous

superstition" (from *Twelve Caesars*, "Nero," XVI). The literal meaning of the word "Christian" is "little Christ."

130 CE: The first appearance of what were called *adversus Judaeos* texts, which center on the denigration of the Jewish religion, basically saying that the Christians replace Jews as the favored folk of God.

130 CE: *The Epistle of Barnabas* (Barnabas was a companion of Paul) is first circulated among Christian groups (first appearing in Egypt) as an anti-Jewish essay (many wanted this included in the New Testament, but it was rejected at the Council of Nicaea).

135 CE: The infancy Gospel of Thomas begins to circulate among early Christian groups, which writes about the supernatural powers of Jesus.

The city of Jerusalem is renamed Aelia Capitoline after the last major Jewish revolt by Simon bar Kokhba is squashed.

140 CE: The probable writing of the Gospel of Philip, a Gnostic treatise discovered at Nag Hammadi in 1947, which elaborated between the exoteric and esoteric teachings of Jesus.

About this time, Christian writers began to delineate between literal understandings of Jesus's teachings and allegorical interpretations that study deeper meanings and "hidden" messages sometimes in the form of apocalyptic revelations in the form of prophecies.

144 CE: The earliest Christian philosopher and historian, Marcion of Pontus, claimed that Jesus did not die at his crucifixion, and he is therefore excommunicated from the church in Rome. Emperor Marcus Aurelius sanctions persecutions of Christians in Lyons and Vienne.

150 CE: The Gospel according to the Ebionites circulates among early Christian groups and forms the basis of the beliefs of many "Jewish Christians." But it was rejected for inclusion in the New Testament at the Council of Nicaea. No intact manuscripts exist since this book was ordered destroyed by Constantine, so

we only know of this work through references in other books and pieces found by scholars.

151 CE: The Proto-Gospel of James circulates among early Christian groups, which recounted the existence of Jesus before his human birth and the life of Mary. It was later rejected by the Council of Nicaea.

155 CE: Christian leader and scholar Justin Martyr admits to Roman authorities that the Christ resurrection story was nothing more than the retelling of the Mithraic myths; he writes one of the first Christian "apologies" or defenses titled *First Apology*. The manuscript titled *Justin: Dialogue with Trypho* is written, which recounts a debate in 135 CE between Justin (Christian philosopher) and Trypho (a non-Christian Jewish scholar), was the first historical theological debate on whether or not Jesus was the Jewish messiah.

The arrest and execution of Polycarp, the bishop of Smyma, in Asia Minor (considered the first historical [outside the New Testament] Christian martyr) is recounted in the manuscript titled *The Martyrdom of Polycarp*, which many early Christian groups used in worship.

156 CE: Christianity is declared the state religion in Britain by royal decree by King Lucius, one of the British kings.

160 CE: The most popular Christian writing begins to circulate among Christian communities: *The Shepherd of Hermas*, written by Hermas, mentioned by Paul as part of oral histories (Rom. 16:14), and first written down on this date.

165 CE: The *Epistle of the Apostles* begins to circulate among early Christian groups, which was a postcrucifixion dialogue between Jesus and his apostles that sought to counter the views of Simon Magus and the Gnostics.

165–80 CE: The Plague of Galen. A series of plagues hits much of the Roman Empire. Even though Christians were still persecuted by the government, followers of this sect willingly helped the afflicted in the streets, earning a growing respect from the populace. These acts of unselfishness did much to win converts to the new religion.

170 CE: The first literary attack against Christians by a philosopher named Celsus is written, titled *The True Word*. The movement called Montanism, founded by Montanus, first appears, which was an early Christian belief in which women held prominent leadership positions, the most famous being Maximilla and Priscilla.

175 CE: The height of Gnostic thought, which taught that there is secret wisdom and knowledge to be learned in the depths of Christianity.

176 CE: Athenagoras writes *The Plea for the Christians* (but evidently did not know about the life of Jesus), which was one of the first attempts to support the Christians.

178 CE: *The Gospel of Truth* first circulates among Christian groups. It was a series of essays about Gnosticism, which was banned later by Constantine but was rediscovered in 1947 and 1960 as part of the Nag Hammadi library.

179 CE: The first actual church in England is constructed in Winchester.

180 CE: The oldest Christian document to survive from North Africa, *The Acts of the Scillitan Martyrs*, recounts the trial narrative of twelve Christians by the proconsul Saturninus. The noncanonical book the *Apocryphon of John* first circulates among early Christian groups, which formed an early exposition of Gnostic beliefs; it was widely read by Christian groups but was rejected at the Council of Nicaea and ordered destroyed by Constantine (only to be rediscovered in 1947 as part of the Nag Hammadi library).

The treatise titled *Against the Heresies* by Irenaeus is published, which highlights the differences between orthodox and unorthodox Christian beliefs among early Christian groups. He demands that there be only four approved Gospels since there are four cardinal directions on the compass. Irenaeus probably named the four Gospels as Matthew, Mark, Luke, and John because prior to this date, there were no names attached to these writings. One of the most quoted lines from *Against the Heresies* is "The glory of God is the human person fully alive," which could be a credo for all Christians.

At this time, some Christian communities began to address the topic of apostasy, which is when a person stops attending/believing in Christian meetings. Some Christians believed this was an unpardonable sin.

Celsus authored attacks on Christianity, which shows the early resistance to the emerging religion.

183 CE: *The Acts of Peter* begins to circulate among early Christian groups, which presented several sermons attributed to Peter, who was contested by his nemesis, Simon Magus.

185 CE: The sermon titled *On the Passover* attributed to Bishop Melito of Sardis is circulated among Christian groups, touting the superiority of Christianity to the Jewish faith.

187 CE: Many early Christian groups follow the belief called Adoptionism, which states that Jesus was born a regular human being of biological human parents but was later "adopted" by God as his emissary and prophet on earth.

190 CE: The noncanonical *The Acts of John* first appears among Christian groups.

195 CE: Tertullian writes his *Apology*, which was a satirical look at the way the Roman establishment was persecuting Christians, and he, Cyprian, and Augustine together are considered the fathers of Western churches, even though all three are from North Africa.

199 CE: *The Muratorian Canon* is widely circulated among early Christian groups, which was the first attempt to compose a sacred book or canon of acceptable and orthodox scripture. It included *The Apocalypse of Peter* and *The Shepherd of Hermas* but

rejected writings by early Christian writers such as Marcion, Valentinus, and Basilides.

200 CE: Christian apologist Tertullian writes that Jesus Christ was a spirit or idea—a logos or an incarnation of a preexisting Jesus that existed before His human form and exists after the death of His human form—a magical essence from heaven that did not exist in human form.

First formation of the Neo-Hebrew language, which survives today.

The bishop of Rome starts to gain predominant position as pope for the Catholic faith.

The First Thought in Three Forms (sometimes called the *Trimorphic Protennoia*) is first circulated among early Christian groups, which inculcated early Gnostic beliefs. It was banned by Constantine and rediscovered in 1947 as part of the Nag Hammadi library.

201 CE: *The Acts of Paul* begins to circulate among early Christian groups, which included a letter of 3 Corinthians and in part described Paul's martyrdom.

202 CE: The circulation of a narrative titled *The Letter of Peter to James and Its Reception*, which was ostensibly a letter written by Peter to Jesus's brother James, the bishop of Jerusalem, opposing the works of Paul, who supported the Christian baptism of non-Jews, based on an oral history handed down over 150 years.

203 CE: The narrative titled *The Martyrdom of Perpetua and Felicitas* (a noncanonical book) first appears, retelling the story of a Roman citizen named Perpetua and her slave named Felicitas who were both executed for being Christians.

204 CE: *The Acts of Thecla* begins to circulate among early Christian groups, which tells the story of a woman converted to Christianity by Paul and who eventually became one of the first female martyrs. It was not included in the New Testament at the Council of Nicaea.

206 CE: *The Didascalia* is written, which describes the qualifications, duties, and conduct of persons holding various offices in the church (including bishops, presbyters, deacons, and readers) and addresses aspects of the early liturgy and the role of women in the church.

208 CE: Tertullian becomes a Montanist.

212 CE: Emperor Catacalla issues the constitution antoniniana, which makes all free men citizens of the Roman Empire, including all Christian men.

215 CE: The *Gospel of Thomas* circulates among early Christian groups as a Gnostic interpretation of Jesus's teachings, which was rejected for inclusion into the New Testament later at the Council of Nicaea. In the Gnostic *Apocryphon of John*, a vision of God appears, saying, "I am the Father, I am the Mother, I am the Child," which some scholars believe would later be incorporated into Christian belief as "Father, Holy Spirit, and Son."

218 CE: Christian communities meet secretly in caves, in catacombs under town streets, in forest clearings at night, and in secluded rooms all over the Roman Empire, sharing the oral histories passed down to them from their leaders, travelers, or memorized letters; in this way, the early Christians forged a new religion.

220 CE: The noncanonical *Acts of Thomas* first appears among Christian groups.

The *Apostolic Tradition* is published by Greek theologian Hippolytus, which formed a template for the organization of the early Catholic Church that, for example, allowed a new convert to participate in Communion only after a rigorous program of teaching, confession, and harsh discipline.

By this year, most of the larger Christian groups are treating the four Gospels and thirteen Pauline epistles as their New Testament.

232 CE: Bishop Heraclas of Alexandria is the first Christian bishop to use the term pope, which means father.

240 CE: The high point of what was called Arianism (later called subordinationism), which stated a belief that Jesus did not exist from the start of the universe or before the creation of the universe but was a later invention by God.

250 CE: Emperor Decius is the first Roman ruler to prescribe a law actually outlawing Christians.

The Christian apologist Origen writes *Against Celsus*, which refutes the anti-Christian essay *The True Word*, written eighty years earlier. Origen writes the *Hexapla*, which was a codex that presented the six versions of early Greek and Hebrew Christian texts side by side so that scholars might spot and resolve inconsistencies. Origen was one of the first theologians who talked about scripture having a literal and historical meaning, although this interpretation was only for "simple believers of simple mind" and those with more maturity and intellectual prowess could grasp scripture's deeper meanings. This more intense dimension of understanding scripture was through allegory, or words meaning other than what is said. Many Christian religions are literalist denominations while other theological students investigate the complexities of what is written.

258 CE: The emergence of Middle Platonism, which becomes a philosophical and theological synergy between Christianity and traditional Greek philosophy, especially focusing on the "supreme good" in the world. Stoicism, the Greek philosophy that there is unity in all of creation, begins to be incorporated into Christian thought.

260 CE: The *Coptic Apocalypse of Peter* circulates among Christian groups, recorded in the first person (Peter). It recounts a series of visions given by Jesus to Peter.

The first *Edict of Toleration* of Christianity is issued by Emperor Gallienus, partly out of respect for the Christian community that helped the poor and sick throughout the empire.

265 CE: The *Second Treatise of the Great Seth* circulates among early Christians as a narrative of a firsthand description by Jesus of

how he descended into the human form. It was rejected for inclusion into the New Testament at the Council of Nicaea.

Early Christians distinguish between full members who have undergone a testing period and baptism and newer converts called catechumen who have yet to be baptized or initiated into the community.

270 CE: The height of Sabellianism, after a Roman priest, Sabellius, which stated that Jesus was only a temporary manifestation of God and never existed separately from God.

269 CE: A man named Anthony in Egypt becomes one of the first famous Christian hermits, also known as one of the first Coptic Christian leaders, establishing what were known as cocnobite communities.

274 CE: Emperor Aurelian declares Mithraism as the first official Roman religion. The worship of Mithras became one of the earliest religious competitors with Christianity, and many of the tenets of Mithraism (i.e., the virgin birth and the December 25 date, etc.) were later adopted by Christian leaders to encourage conversion.

280 CE: Christian writers begin to discuss the concept of atonement, which teaches that God preplanned the torture and death of his son Jesus so that humanity (under the yoke of the original sin of Adam and Eve) might find a means to be reconciled with God.

290 CE: Five percent of the Roman Empire identify themselves as Christians.

295 CE: The Syrian Christian leader Tatian creates the *Diatessaron*, which combined the four Gospels into one codex or book, and it was used by Syrian Christians for centuries.

305 CE: Council of Elvira, attended by most bishops, bans marriage between Jews and Christians and between pagans and Christians and bans Jews eating in the same room as Christians. Christians enact prohibitions against clerics marrying.

311 CE: Roman officials under the guidance of Constantine enact the second Edict of Toleration, which promises religious freedom to Christians. The Edict of Milan (313) gives freedom to all Romans to worship as they please, but Christians refused to allow for other beliefs.

Eusebius publishes his version of the first history of early Christianity, which forms the earliest "orthodox" views of Christian history.

314 CE: The Council of Ancyra, attended by many bishops, orders Christians to torture and murder non-Christian priests and pagan clerics and orders the demolition of pagan temples. The bishops wrestled with the confusing interpretations of what exactly was the "Holy Spirit," which was not being taught consistently throughout the various communities.

317 CE: Christian Catholic militarists murder Christian Donatists who believe that Jesus was not God but (following John 1:3) was made by God to be an instrument by which the world was created.

320 CE: Construction begins on the first Church of St. Peter in Rome.

324 CE: Constantine defeats Lucinius and emerges as the emperor over both the East and West.

325 CE: Council of Nicaea is called by Constantine to unify various Christian beliefs into one accepted theology. The adoption of the Nicene Creed, the deletion of many early Christian books from the orthodox canon, and the establishment of the calendar date of Easter occurred. The building of the Church of the Nativity in Bethlehem begins. The belief of many Christians that Jesus was divine and only appeared to be in human form, called Docetism, was rejected by the Nicaean Council, and its believers were treated as heretics and killed off. The Ebionites who believed that Jesus was not a divinity and who did not believe in his virgin birth were branded as heretics and killed off. The council also used the term homoousios (of the same substance) to refer

to the relationship between God and Jesus (to be distinguished from homoios [like] and homoiousios [like in substance]), which was variously taught in different Christian communities. After the council, to teach anything other than homoousios became a heresy. Many Christian communities had started to believe in tritheism (the idea that there are three distinct divinities instead of the orthodox view of trinity), which was rejected by the council, and the tritheists were branded as heretics.

326 CE: At the direction of his mother, Helena, Constantine destroys temples of the traditional pagan gods and goddesses. The same year he murders his firstborn son, Crispus, and kills his wife by steaming her to death. He then sponsors excursions to the Holy Land (discovering thousands of "icons," "relics," and "artifacts" associated with Jesus and his disciples and apostles, sending them to newly built churches all over Europe).

Building begins on the Church of the Holy Sepulchre in Jerusalem.

328 CE: Byzantium is given a new name, Constantinople, and made the new capital of the Roman Empire.

330 CE: Constantine orders Roman temples plundered.

The first Basilican Church of St. Peter's is built; it was demolished in 1506 and then the present building was erected.

335 CE: Constantine orders the crucifixion of all non-Christian magicians and soothsayers.

337 CE: Constantine is finally baptized, and he dies. He is buried in the Church of the Apostles and is given the title The Thirteenth Disciple by Christian leaders.

346 CE: Christian bishops order the violent persecution of all non-Christians in Constantinople.

353 CE: Constantine II orders all non-Christian temples closed and turned into brothels or gambling establishments.

359 CE: Christians in Skythopolis (Syria) organize death camps for the torture and execution of non-Christians from around the empire. Tens of thousands of non-Christians perish.

364 CE: The Eastern monastic order is established by Basil the Great, which emphasized koinobios (living in a community). This countered the idea of a solitary life taught by the anchorite Christians, thus forming the template for future monastic orders. Basil, along with Gregory of Nazianzus and Gregory of Nyssa, are referred to as the Cappadocian Fathers who helped formulate the concept of the Trinity.

367 CE: The first Christian canon (in fact, this is the first year the word "canon," kanonizomena, is used) is assembled into twenty-seven New Testament books by Athanasius in his Easter Letter.

370 CE: Emperor Valens orders the persecution of non-Christians throughout the empire.

372 CE: Valens orders the destruction of all noncanonical Christian writings.

374 CE: Ambrose, bishop of Milan, writes *On the Duties of the Clergy*, which became an ethical teaching for priests and was one of the first to urge the devotion of Mary as the mother of Jesus.

376 CE: The Catholic Church seizes the Mithraeum on Vatican Hill in the name of Jesus Christ on December 25, the birthday of Mithras.

380–81 CE: Emperor Theodosius I decrees that all wills of non-Christians would be illegal, so only Christians could inherit or bequeath property in the empire, thus establishing Christianity as the only official religion in the Western empire. He also is the first to officially decree the existence of the Trinity.

386 CE: Jerome begins the task of translating the four Gospels and Paul's epistles into Latin, which forms the basis of the Vulgate Bible, which became the most widely used holy book by priests in the West.

388 CE: Theodosian laws make it illegal to disagree with the church.

391 CE: By decree, Emperor Theodosius elevates Jesus to divinity, declaring Christianity as the only official Roman religion under penalty of death.

Also, this year, Christians storm the libraries at Serapeum, Alexandria, and Mithraeum and destroy many remaining books of antiquity (original writings of Euripides, Sophocles, Aeschylus, Plato, Ptolemy, Aristotle, and many thousands of others), including the histories and papers and scrolls of early Christianity. This pushes the Roman Empire into the Dark Ages. A Christian church was constructed over the site of the great library at Serapeum.

393 CE: Council of Hippo. The Roman Catholic Church urges the destruction of all noncanonical writings.

397 CE: Council of Carthage declares the canonization of the Bible into the recognized books of the Old and New Testaments. The early church starts to divide the year into seasonal observances such as Advent, Christmas, Epiphany, Lent, Easter, Pentecost, and Ordinary Time.

398 CE: The Fourth Council of Carthage forbids bishops from reading nonbiblical writings.

405 CE: John Chrysostom's army of Christian monks destroys non-Christian temples and pagan idols in Palestine, somewhat planting the seeds that will grow into the split between the orthodox and Roman Catholics.

408 CE: Western Empire Emperor Honorius and Eastern Empire Emperor Arcadius order all non-Christian sculptures and idols destroyed throughout the world.

411 CE: Augustine's book *The City of God* is published posthumously after the sack of Rome by the pagan Alaric. The book first officially lays out the concepts of "original sin" and "grace" as reasons for Jesus's crucifixion.

415 CE: The pope of Alexandria, Saint Cyril, orders the arrest and torture of (sixty-year-old) Hypatia, the librarian of the Library of Serapeum (which was destroyed in 391) who was teaching philosophy and science. She was stripped naked, dragged through streets, and skinned alive. Then the Catholic monks chopped up her body and burned it.

418 CE: With the excommunication by the Roman Catholic Church of Pelagius, the church henceforth held the doctrine of hereditary transmission of original sin down through every generation since Adam. Only through following Jesus could this original sin be erased.

429 CE: Emperor Theodosius II declares all non-Christian religions around the world to be "demon worship," and all non-Christians were to be tortured and imprisoned.

432 CE: Patrick begins his mission to Ireland.

435 CE: Theodosius II orders the death penalty for all non-Christians around the world, excluding Jews.

438 CE: All Christian heretics not adhering to orthodoxy are ordered killed.

448 CE: The Roman government orders the burning of all non-Christian books.

450 CE: Bishop Theodore of Cyrrhus writes that there were over two hundred different Gospels circulating in his diocese alone.

451 CE: The Council of Chalcedon exempts priests from military service, shields all bishops against criminal charges, and forbids marriages between priests and nuns.

The doctrine of monophysitism (the dual nature of Jesus) is prohibited, resulting in the excommunication of members of Coptic Christianity and the Christian church in Ethiopia, Eritrea, India, and Armenia.

Marriage elopements are prohibited in all of Christendom.

480 CE: Benedict of Nursia is born, who eventually serves as the patriarch of Western monasticism (dies in 543).

Benedictine Order established in 529.

482–89 CE: Virtually all non-Christians are killed in Asia Minor.

484–519 CE: The first schism of the orthodox Christian church and the Roman Catholics happens when Pope Felix II excommunicates Patriarch Acacius of Constantinople.

491 CE: The Armenian church secedes from the Roman Catholic and orthodox arenas.

499 CE: The Roman Catholic Church sets forth its first organized process for the election of popes.

500 CE: Incense is first introduced in Christian church services.

527 CE: Emperors Justin and Justinian order that the property of all non-Christians be confiscated.

528 CE: Justinian orders that all pagans, sorcerers, magicians, and "baptized persons who follow pagan or nonorthodox practices" be put to death.

529 CE: Justinian orders the closing of all non-Christian schools of philosophy and all non-Christian institutions. Thousands of non-Christians and Christian heretics are tortured and murdered.

550 CE: In France, church bells appear for the first time.

570 CE: Muhammed, founder of Islam, is born.

583 CE: Theodosius orders the murder of tens of thousands of pagans.

590 CE: In Tours, France, stained glass is used in churches for the first time.

599 CE: Pope Gregory proclaims that Jews are "Christ killers," resulting in the murder of millions of Jews in various pogroms in the next millennia and a half.

602 CE: The archiepiscopal see of Canterbury is established.

610 CE: The first use of episcopal rings is seen among members of the Catholic Church hierarchy.

633 CE: The Fourth Council of Toledo prohibits Jews from holding office or owning Christian slaves.

The Holy Lands fall under Islamic control.

680 CE: The monothelite controversy/debate had existed since the earliest days of the church, questioning whether Jesus possessed a divine will and/or a human will. Monothelites stated that he could not have both. The controversy was eventually settled by

the Sixth Council of Constantinople: Jesus did have both divine and human will.

700 CE: Easter eggs first appear among Christian cultures.

710 CE: Justinian II is the first monarch to kiss the foot of the pope, thus signifying papal rule over political leadership.

756 CE: Pepin grants the pope temporal rule over Rome, creating the Papal States.

768 CE: Constantine III becomes the first antipope.

783 CE: In one day, Charlemagne beheads forty-five hundred Saxons at Verdun for refusing to be baptized.

787 CE: Seventh Council of Nicaea regulates image worship and makes icons and relics official.

800 CE: Pope Leo II separates from the orthodox church in the East and becomes supreme bishop in the West for the Roman Catholic Church.

845 CE: The Vivian Bible, one of the earliest illustrated bibles, is written in Tours.

848 CE: Pope Leo IV has the Leonine Wall built around Vatican Hill.

850 CE: Jews settling in Germany begin to develop their own language: Yiddish.

879 CE: The pope and the patriarch of Constantinople excommunicate each other.

895 CE: The earliest transcript in Hebrew of the Old Testament is produced, in its present format.

913 CE: Pope Lando is the last pope to have an original name; henceforth all popes assume a name used by a predecessor.

1022 CE: Start of the Cathar persecution in France. Cathars were devout and peaceful Christians who were believers in a non-orthodox theology. They were murdered by armies of the Roman Catholics. Over a two-hundred-year period, over one million Cathars were killed in a religious genocide, referred to in history as the Albigensian genocide.

1059 CE: Papal elections by cardinals only.

1074 CE: Excommunication of married priests.

1096 CE: The First Christian Crusade starts to wrest the Holy Lands from Muslim control following the Council of Clermont preached by Pope Urban II.

1099 CE: The Jerusalem Massacre, in which Christian crusaders kill tens of thousands of Muslims. Over the course of the next one hundred years, European Christians would create several wars of conquest or crusades resulting in the death of hundreds of thousands of Muslims.

1128 CE: Order of Knights Templar is recognized by the pope.

1155 CE: Carmelite order is founded.

1163 CE: Notre Dame in Paris is built.

1170 CE: Pope Alexander II establishes rules for the canonization of saints.

1187 CE: Under the military leadership of Islamic Sultan Saladin, Muslim armies recapture Jerusalem, and Christians are booted out of the Holy Lands.

1198 CE: Pope Innocent II declares that any layperson who reads the Bible should be stoned to death.

1209 CE: Francis of Assisi issues first rules for the Franciscan order.

1212 CE: The so-called Children's Crusade, in which over fifty thousand children and youth mounted a march through Italy to somehow acquire ships with which to sail to the Holy Lands to wrestle control back from Islam. The children were mostly captured at the town of Brindisi located on Italy's "boot" and sold into slavery or died from starvation.

1213 CE: The Fifth Crusade, promoted by Innocent III, fails.

1215 CE: The Fourth Lateran Council of the Roman Catholic Church calls for the extermination of Christians who were heretics, resulting in the genocide of tens of thousands of Christians. This council is also known for changing the meaning of the Eucharist

(Protestants call this Communion) by inventing the concept of transubstantiation, which decreed that the bread and wine at the shared table in worship actually (really, in reality) becomes the flesh and blood of Jesus. Most Protestants believe this to be only metaphorical. Prior to this time, there were varied interpretations regarding the meaning of this activity.

Eventually, Pope Honorius III decreed that all Jews had to wear special badges when in public, and Jews were banned from holding public office in Europe.

1228 CE: The Sixth Crusade against Islam fails.

1229 CE: The Roman Catholic Council of Toulouse prohibits the ownership of a Bible by a layperson under penalty of death. Nobody but a cleric can read a Bible.

1233 CE: Thirty thousand Christians living in Germany, called Stedingers, are killed by Roman Catholic armies in a crusade to wipe out unorthodox belief.

1248 CE: The Seventh Crusade, led by Louis IX of France, fails.

1252 CE: Pope Innocent IV orders the arrest, torture, and death of so-called witches. More than one million men, women, children, and animals are murdered over the next six hundred years in Europe as witches.

1270 CE: The Eighth Crusade ends in failure.

1272 CE: The Ninth Crusade ends in failure.

1302 CE: The supremacy of the pope is recognized in all theological law in Catholic countries.

1309 CE: Clement V (a Frenchman) fixes the papal residence at Avignon, starting the Babylonian Captivity, during which Rome is not the papal seat.

1314 CE: Jacques DeMolay, grand master of the Knights Templar, is burned at the stake, and the property of that order is confiscated by King Philip of France.

1377 CE: The Babylonian Captivity ends when Pope Gregory XI returns to Rome.

1378 CE: The great schism starts with two or more popes existing at the same time; it ended in 1409 at the Council of Pisa with the election of Pope Alexander V.

1382 CE: John Wycliff translates the Bible into English, and when he dies, the Catholic Church declares him a heretic. His books were burned and his body was posthumously dug up and burned. Bibles could only exist in Latin during the Dark Ages.

1450 CE: Johannes Gutenberg begins to mass-produce the Vulgate Bible in Latin.

1452 CE: Pope Nicholas V decrees in a Papal Bull to begin the European slave trade, eventually enslaving millions of Africans, Muslims, and pagans.

Widespread sale of indulgences by priests (in which Catholics might buy their way out of purgatory).

1480 CE: The start of the infamous Catholic Inquisition in Spain, resulting in the murders of tens of thousands.

1491 CE: Birth of Ignatius Loyola, founder of the Jesuit Order.

1492 CE: Columbus begins his four voyage expeditions to Christianize the New World, resulting in the genocide of six million Native Americans.

1499 CE: Moors in Spain are ordered to die or convert to Christianity, starting the great Moorish Revolt.

1501 CE: Martin Luther, the founder of Lutheranism and leader of the Protestant movement, is born.

1509 CE: John Calvin is born.

Emperor Maximilian orders the destruction of all Jewish books in Germany.

1512 CE: The Fifth Lateran Council declares that the soul of a Christian lives forever.

1517 CE: Luther posts his ninety-five theses on the door of Palast Church in Wittenberg, thus starting the Reformation.

1520 CE: Luther is excommunicated, and two years later, Luther begins to publish the Bible in languages other than Latin.

1525 CE: Luther marries former nun Katherine von Bora.

1527 CE: The first Protestant university is founded at Marburg.

1536 CE: An act of Parliament declares the power of the pope is void in England.

1541 CE: John Knox leads the Calvinist Reformation in Scotland.

Sixteenth century: The start of Protestantism by Martin Luther.

1545–63 CE: Over thirty thousand versions of the Bible are in use throughout the world, so the Council of Trent is held. The first stable form of the Christian Bible is finalized.

1555 CE: The Old and New Testaments are divided into the recognizable chapters and verses with numbers found in almost all Bibles today; prior to this date, these scripture distinctions did not exist.

1562–98 CE: The French Wars of Religion between the Protestant Huguenots and Catholics result in the death of four million people.

1564 CE: The Catholic Church condemns the owning of books by Luther, Zwingli, Calvin, and other Protestants.

Seventeenth century: Roman Catholic tribunals prohibit belief in the Copernican Theory that the planets circle the sun. Believers are tortured and killed.

1618–48 CE: The Thirty Years War between Protestants and Catholics results in the death of eight million people—Christians killing Christians.

1632 CE: The Catholic Church declares Galileo's ideas contradictory to Christian belief.

1641 CE: Thirty thousand Christians die at the hands of other Christians in the Irish Rebellion.

1648 CE: Bishop James Ussher recalculates the age of the universe as starting on October 23, 4004 BCE. Many Christians today believe in this timeline.

1844 CE: The "year of the great disappointment" as several "prophets," such as William Miller, had predicted through researching the Bible that the world would end; but it did not this year, giving rise to many new Christian religions such as the Seventh Day Adventist sect.

1851–64 CE: The Taiping Rebellion, between followers of Hong Ziuquan who said he was a relative and follower of Jesus and other Chinese people, resulting in the death of fifty million people.

1854 CE: Pope Pius X issues a declaration that Mary, mother of Jesus, was born free from original sin and that she remained a virgin her whole life as the doctrine of the Immaculate Conception.

1929 CE: The Lateran Treaty between Mussolini and the pope established Vatican City as a sovereign nation belonging to the Catholic Church.

1933–45 CE: The Holocaust is perpetrated on the Jewish population of Europe by Christians of the Third Reich. Over six million Jews are killed.

1946–47 CE: The Dead Sea Scrolls are unearthed in caves in Qumran by the Dead Sea, twelve miles from Bethlehem.

1992–95 CE: Ethnic cleansing in the name of Christianity takes place in Bosnia, resulting in the death of one hundred thousand people.

Twenty-first century: renewed efforts around the world to find Christian unity.

FURTHER READING

Alter, Robert, and Frank Kermode. *The Literary Guide to the Bible.* Cambridge, MA: Harvard University Press, 1987.

Armstrong, Karen. *Holy War: The Crusades and Their Impact on Today's World.* New York: Doubleday, 1988.

Ashe, Geoffrey. *The Virgin: Mary's Cult and the Re-emergence of the Goddess.* London: Arkana Press, 1988.

Backhous, Stephen. *The Compact Guide to Christian History.* Oxford: Lion Hudson, 2011.

Bass, Diana Butler. *Christianity for the Rest of Us.* San Francisco, CA: HarperSanFrancisco, 2006.

Bass, Diana Butler. *A People's History of Christianity.* New York: HarperOne, 1989.

Bossy, John. *Christianity in the West 1400–1700.* Oxford: Oxford University Press, 1985.

Brock, Rita Nakashima, and Rebecca Ann Parker. *Saving Paradise: How Christianity Traded Love of This World for Crucifixion and Empire.* Boston, MA: Boston Beacon Press, 2008.

Brown, Raymond E. *The Death of the Messiah: A Commentary on the Passion Narratives in the Four Gospels* (two volumes). New York: Doubleday, 1994.

Carpenter, Edward. *Pagan and Christian Creeds: Their Origin and Meaning.* Sioux Falls, SD: NuVision, 2007.

Chancey, Mark A. *The Myth of a Gentile Galilee.* Cambridge: Cambridge University Press, 2002.

Chilton, Bruce, and Craig A. Evans. *James the Just and Christian Origins.* Leiden: Brill Press, 1999.

Chin, Shunshin, and Joshua A. Fogel. *The Taiping Rebellion.* London: Harper Collins, 1982.

Clauss, Manfred. *The Roman Cult of Mithras.* New York: Routledge, 2001.

Comfort, Philip W., and David P. Barrett, eds. *Complete Text of the Earliest New Testament Manuscripts.* Grand Rapids, MI: Baker Publishing, 1999.

Crossan, John Dominic. *The Birth of Christianity: Discovering What Happened in the Years Immediately After the Execution of Jesus.* San Francisco, CA: HarperSanFrancisco, 1998.

Davis, Stevan. "Mark's Use of the Gospel of Thomas." *Neotestamentica: The Journal of the New Testament Society of South Africa* 30, no. 2 (1996): 307–34.

Doan, Thomas William. *Bible Myths and Their Parallels in Other Religions.* New York: Cosimo Classics, 2007.

Dobson, C. C. *Did Our Lord Visit Britain as They Say in Cornwall and Somerset?* Ninth Revised Edition. London: Covenant Publishing, 2008.

Dungan, David L. *Constantine's Bible.* Minneapolis, MN: Fortress Press, 2007.

Dzielska, Maria. *Apollonius of Tyana in Legend and History.* Cambridge, MA: Harvard University Press, 1986.

Ehrman, Bart. *After the New Testament.* Oxford: Oxford University Press, 1999.

Ehrman, Bart. *Jesus Before the Gospels: How the Earliest Christians Remembered, Changed, and Invented Their Stories of the Savior.* New York: HarperOne, 2016.

Ehrman, Bart. *Jesus Interrupted.* London: Harper Collins, 2009.

Ehrman, Bart. *Lost Christianities.* Oxford: Oxford University Press, 2003.

Ehrman, Bart. *Lost Scriptures.* Oxford: Oxford University Press, 2003.

Ehrman, Bart. *Misquoting Jesus.* London: Harper Collins, 2006.

Ehrman, Bart. *The New Testament: A Historical Introduction to the Early Christian Writings.* Oxford: Oxford University Press, 2004.

Ehrman, Bart. *Orthodox Corruption of Scripture*. Oxford: Oxford University Press, 1997.

Ellingsen, Mark. *Reclaiming Our Roots: An Inclusive Introduction to Church History*. Harrisburg, PA: Trinity Press, 1999.

Freeman, Charles. *A New History of Early Christianity*. New Haven, CT: Yale University Press, 2009.

Grant, Michael. *Jesus: A Historian's Review of the Gospels*. New York: Scribner, 1995.

Gower, Ralph. *The New Manners and Customs of Bible Times*. Chicago, IL: Moody Press, 1987.

Hardwick, Michael. *Josephus as an Historical Source in Patristic Literature through Eusebius*. Brown Judaic Studies. Atlanta, GA: Scholars Press, 1989.

Jenkins, Philip. *The Lost History of Christianity*. New York: HarperOne, 2008.

Jeremias, Joachiml. *Jerusalem in the Time of Jesus*. London: SCM Press, 1969.

Lüdemann, Gerd. *The Resurrection of Christ: A Historical Inquiry*. Amherst, NY: Promethean Books, 2004.

Maaffie, Barbara. *Her Story: Women in Christian Tradition*. Philadelphia, PA: Fortress Press, 1986.

Mack, Burton. *The Lost Gospel: The Book of Q and Christian Origins*. London: Harper Collins, 1993.

Mason, Steve. *Josephus and the New Testament*. Peabody, MA: Hendrickson Publishers, 1992.

Massey, Gerald. *Gnostic and Historic Christianity*. Whitefish, MT: Kessinger Publishing, 2005.

McBirnie, William Steuart. *The Search for the Twelve Apostles*. Wheaton, IL: Tyndale House Publishers, Revised Edition, 2004.

Paulkovich, Michael. *No Meek Messiah*. Annapolis, MD: Spillax Publishers, 2012.

Peterson, Eugene H. *The Message: The Bible in Contemporary Language*. Colorado Springs, CO: NavPress Publishing Group, 2002.

Price, Dennis. *The Missing Years of Jesus: The Greatest Story Never Told.* Carlsbad, CA: Hay House Publishing, 2009.

Putnam, Robert D. *Bowling Alone.* New York: Simon & Schuster, 2001.

Roth, Cecil. *The Spanish Inquisition.* New York: Norton Press, 1964.

Salm, René. *The Myth of Nazareth.* Cranford, NJ: American Press, 2008.

Schweitzer, Albert. *The Quest of the Historical Jesus.* Philadelphia, PA: Fortress Press, 2001.

Smith, David Whitten, and Elizabeth Geraldine Burr. *Understanding World Religions: A Road Map for Justice and Peace.* Lanham, MD: Rowman and Littlefied, 2007.

Stannard, David. *American Holocaust: The Conquest of the New World.* Oxford: Oxford University Press, 1993.

Stark, Rodney. *The Rise of Christianity: A Sociologist Reconsiders History.* Princeton, NJ: Princeton University Press, 1996.

Strachan, Gordon. *Jesus the Master Builder: Druid Mysteries and The Dawn of Christianity.* Edinburgh: Floris Books, 1998.

Thomsett, Michael C. *The Inquisition: A History.* Jefferson, NC: McFarland & Co., 2010.

Tickle, Phyllis. *The Great Emergence: How Christianity Is Changing and Why.* Grand Rapids, MI: Baker Books, 2008.

Trickler, C. Jack. *A Layman's Guide to: Who Wrote the Books of the Bible?* Bloomington, IN: AuthorHouse, 2006.

Tyerman, Christopher. *God's War: A New History of the Crusades.* Cambridge, MA: Harvard University Press, 2006.

Walker, Barbara. *The Women's Encyclopedia of Myths and Secrets.* New York: HarperOne, 1983.

Wedgewood, C. V. *The Thirty Years War.* New York: NYRB Classics, 2005.

Wildinson, Richard H. *The Complete Gods and Goddesses of Ancient Egypt.* London: Thames and Hudson, 2003.

Williams, Rowan. *Why Study the Past? The Quest for the Historical Church.* Grand Rapids, MI: Eerdmans, 2005.

Made in the USA
San Bernardino, CA
27 June 2017